BILLIONAIRE WOLF NEEDS A NANNY

MY GRUMPY WEREWOLF BOSS 1 (A PARANORMAL BAD BOY ROMANCE)

DRUSILLA SWAN

MY GRUMPY WEREWOLF BOSS SERIES

These grumpy bad boy bosses are impossible to please. That is, except by the one woman who is fated to be his mate. When these werewolf billionaires catch the scent of their mate, they will use all of their power to possess her...

Billionaire Wolf Needs a Nanny (Blake and Lacey)

Billionaire Wolf Needs an Assistant (Reeve and Katie)

Billionaire Wolf Needs a Fake Girlfriend (Denver and Sasha)

INTRODUCTION

Book 1 of the My Grumpy Werewolf Boss series

Lacey has bigger dreams than being a nanny for the Discreet Talent Connections Agency, but rent needs to be paid and desperate times call for desperate measures. Besides, the job is only supposed to last one year, and the financial reward will make it possible for her to fulfill her dream of publishing her novel. The little girl she is in charge of is wild, but sweet. The child's uncle, and guardian, on the other hand is a grumpy bachelor wolf shifter who both infuriates her and ignites her senses on fire.

Blake Wulfthorn is on the cusp of landing the biggest acquisition of his life. But being the sole guardian of his orphaned niece threatens to derail his plans, unless he finds a nanny who can handle an energetic wolf pup. The last person he expected the employment agency to send, was a woman with sharp eyes behind heavy glasses, and curves in all the right places. A human woman is only another distraction from his role as CEO and his duties to his wolf pack. She fits in his

INTRODUCTION

family and his life perfectly in almost every way except one. She was human, and his employee, and 100% off limits. Is he willing to risk it all for the one who could be his mate?

This is a standalone story with a HEA. Each book in the My Grumpy Werewolf Boss series features a new billionaire werewolf MMC and new FMC. All of the books in this series can be read independently in any order.

CHAPTER 1

LACEY

Fat drops of rain fell from heavy gray clouds that covered the sky like a thick blanket. It had been pouring nonstop all morning, and everything was slick and drenched.

With a high-pitched screech, a car pulled up from behind, spraying a cascade of rainwater from the puddles on the road that landed across the sidewalk. I leaped out of the way, pressing myself against the door of a nearby shop. It was no use, and I still ended up with dirty water soaking through my boots and jeans.

My heart thudded in my chest, and I wanted to shake my fist at the car, but it was no use. As it vanished into the distance, the car's bass rattled the road with its rhythmic thud. The driver inside was oblivious to the chaos he left behind him.

Everybody else on the sidewalk walked past me at a brisk pace, paying the car no mind. The first thing I noticed when I first moved here was that everybody was in a hurry to get to their destination. Was this what it was like to live in the big city? Was I going to eventually become numb to the daily indignities I would encounter on the streets?

On the other side of the road, tucked in between the towering glass skyscrapers of downtown Huntington Harbor, I spotted my target. The cozy little coffee shop was barely bigger than a shack. After an entire morning of walking around in the rain, the inviting glow from inside and the familiar coffee bean logo announced the shop as a port of safe harbor for weary commuters. Bean Brewing and Sipping's chain of shops was always a welcoming place to hang out. It didn't matter if I was in a small town in the middle of Nebraska or a bustling city like Huntington Harbor.

As soon as the light at the crosswalk turned, I dashed from the shop doorway and ran across the road. A bell over the door let out a tinkling ring as I stepped inside. The warm interior was a sharp contrast to the bone-chilling humidity outside.

Safe inside, I finally noticed that the icy rain had completely soaked through my clothes to the skin. Even the calming jazz music that floated through the air was not enough to muffle the wet squelching sound my shoes let out with each step I took.

"Welcome to Bean Brewing and Sipping," announced the barista behind the counter. "Customers are welcome to use our restroom. You can freshen up and wait here until the rain lets up." She shot me a pitying look. "Huntington Harbor is famous for flash rainstorms. It'll be over and sunny outside before you know it."

"Is it that obvious that I'm new to the city?" I thought I fit in so well with the other residents in the city. One of the first things I did after I arrived in Huntington Harbor and moved in with my roommate, Katie, was to buy new clothes to replace my dated wardrobe from back home. Looking down, I judged my outfit. I was wearing a pair of loose jeans and a designer leather jacket that Katie and I had found for twenty bucks at a thrift store.

The barista smiled. "It's the shocked and confused look on your face. Don't worry, we've all been there."

I shot her a weak smile, embarrassed that my status as a country bumpkin radiated like bad body odor.

I glanced around the coffee shop. Despite this location's notoriety as the chain's first location, it was oddly empty except for a few customers. At the far end of the dining room against the back wall, a tall intimidating man sat alone. He was busy working on his laptop. The cup on his table was empty and the beverage it had contained was long consumed, leaving the top of it lined with a dried ring of coffee-stained milk foam. Two empty crumpled packets of sugar were on the table next to the cup.

He was good-looking, with broad shoulders and a strong muscular body that filled his perfectly tailored gray suit. His dark hair was clean cut and every strand was styled into place. I would have said he was handsome, except he was burning a hole into me with his fiery copper eyes. He reminded me of a predator, like a wolf or mountain lion stalking his prey.

I probably disrupted him from whatever work he was doing on his computer. Power and arrogance radiated off him in waves. The guy looked like a stuck-up finance bro who worked in one of the towering office buildings next door. On his wrist, he wore a large silver watch that I guessed was worth more than an entire house. I resisted the urge to roll my eyes. His type, as I already discovered, was a dime a dozen in the city. They acted like they were gods and looked down on anybody who didn't make as much money as them. People like me.

Ignoring him, I walked over to the counter. "Let's see, I'll have a flat white, please."

I paid for the order and the barista slid the key to the restroom across the counter.

"Your order will be ready in a couple of minutes. The restroom is down the stairs to your right."

I muttered my thanks and disappeared in the direction she indicated. Thankfully, the restroom was a private room instead of a row of stalls. Glancing at my reflection in the mirror, I cringed at the drowned rat staring back at me. I looked like I had just crawled out of the sewers. No wonder the asshole out there was judging me so hard.

Pulling a wad of paper towels from the dispenser, I wiped the droplets of rain that clung to my glasses. Then, as best as I could, I toweled my hair and neck before wringing the water out from my shirt. What I couldn't get out, I tried to dry with the blowing hand dryer. My shoes were a lost cause though. What a pity. I really liked the ankle-length suede boots. Not that it mattered much, since I was going straight home as soon as the rain stopped.

The only reason I had to brave the horrible weather and come downtown was to record my employment interview and sign some forms at Discreet Talent Connections Agency. All of the agency's clients were powerful people and celebrities who had little time to find their own employees. A posting from the agency was my best bet at a job that paid enough to cover the bills.

Signing up to become a personal assistant for some rich businessman wasn't what I had planned on doing with my life, but I needed money. I couldn't mooch off Katie without chipping in for my share of the rent. Besides, living off instant ramen and frozen peas was quickly losing its novelty. This situation was only temporary. All I wanted was a well-paid job that didn't demand too much of me mentally and covered my living expenses while I finished writing my paranormal romance novel.

By the time I stepped back out into the dining room, my order was waiting for me at the counter. The rich nutty aroma of the freshly brewed coffee hit my nose. I picked up the cup with care, making sure the coffee didn't slosh over the lip and admired the latte art of a heart on the surface.

Maybe I should train to be a barista? Working in a coffee shop seemed like it would be fun. I shook my head. Knowing how clumsy and forgetful I was, I could already picture myself scalding my hand with hot steam from the espresso machine and mixing up everybody's orders.

I turned around to find somewhere to sit, only to let out a yelp as I crashed into somebody. My coffee tumbled out of my hand and splattered all over the crisp gray silk suit of the man who was standing right behind me.

The coffee had to be scalding hot, but he didn't even flinch as it soaked through his shirt and suit. Some of it splashed back onto my jacket before dripping onto my boots. Great. Just what I needed.

It was the guy who had been staring at me when I entered the coffee shop. I hadn't heard him make a single noise. How did he sneak up so close to me?

He put his hands on my shoulders to steady me. "Is it a custom in Oklahoma to go around tossing your coffee at strangers?"

"Only those who sneak up on me like a creeper." Ignoring the warmth of his hands seeping through my jacket, I shrugged off his grip.

"And I'm from Nebraska, not Oklahoma," I growled. The speed with which he identified me as an out-of-towner only flamed my anger.

He looked down his sharp nose at me, scanning his judgmental gaze up and down my figure. "Same difference."

I balled my fists. Arrogant jerk.

Up close, he was even bigger and more intimidating than he seemed from across the room. My nose was right at his chest level. He had wide shoulders that made him seem like a brick wall. Not that I was going to let him intimidate me. His eyes shimmered with amusement as I refused to step back. I had no doubt that he expected me to apologize for the accident.

"You need to watch your step before you piss off the wrong person, or you're not going to last very long in Huntington Harbor."

Was that a threat? Before I could even process his words, he picked up his laptop from the table behind him and walked out of the door. How strange. From the large front window, I watched him make his way down the sidewalk and disappear into the crowd.

The barista rushed over and handed me a bunch of paper napkins. "Oh my. Let me make you a fresh cup."

I dabbed at the coffee on my jacket. "No, that's okay. It's my fault, and I've already caused enough trouble for you." I gestured toward the window where a beam of sunlight spilled into the coffee shop. "Besides, the rain has already stopped, just like you said it would."

On the hour-long bus ride back home, I stewed in my anger and coffee-soaked clothes. What a jerk! The nerve of that man to threaten me after he was the one who invaded my space.

I got off at the bus stop near my apartment. As usual, the front door of the building was jammed shut. The lock had been broken for as long as I lived here, so the sticky door was actually the only security measure we had against strangers wandering into the building. I kicked the door repeatedly until it finally popped open.

Junk mail littered the entryway, which meant the mailman had already been here this morning. Our mailbox was filled with the usual, ads and bills. Not that I expected anything else. Well, a check from an unknown millionaire aunt would have been nice, but the chance of an inheritance coming my way was as likely to happen as getting struck by lightning.

When I opened the door and stepped into the living room, Katie was sitting on the floor behind the coffee table and buried up to her chest in a pile of yarn balls. We were both in between jobs right now. To make some money, my roommate ran an online store selling crocheted stuffed toys.

Her chestnut hair was tied up in a messy bun and a fuzzy pink headband held back the unruly strands around her face. She was still dressed in her blue penguin pajamas, and it looked like she hadn't moved since I left earlier to go to Huntington Harbor.

I kicked off my wet shoes next to the front door and tossed the bills onto the coffee table before I collapsed on the cheap futon behind her.

"What are you making this time?"

"Baby Yoda sitting in a space pod."

She stuck her hand inside the still unstuffed project and moved her fingers so that the deflated crocheted Yoda nodded at me. Most of the orders she received were for custom fan commissions.

"Cute. Has the agency called you yet?"

Katie stabbed her crochet hook into the project and worked another row of stitches.

"No. I think they've tossed my file into the trash."

I settled into the cushions. My heart sank. Katie was the one who referred me to the agency, and she had joined long before I even submitted my application. If Katie, with her multiple impressive talents, couldn't get a callback, then what hope did I have?

Her crochet hook paused in the middle of the next stitch. Katie sniffed the air and crinkled her nose. "Why do you smell like a wet dog that's rolled in a puddle of coffee?"

"Ugh. Don't even get me started. This whole morning was awful. You wouldn't believe the guy I ran into."

Just then, my phone started ringing in my jacket pocket. I looked at the screen and then at Katie.

"It's the agency."

She tossed aside her crochet project and scrambled up onto the futon next to me. "Well, what are you waiting for? Answer it."

I accepted the call and put it on speaker. As if the person on the other end of the line could see me, I straightened my back and sat primly on the edge of my seat. Clearing my throat, I put on my best professional-sounding voice.

"Hello, this is Lacey Conway speaking."

"Good afternoon, Ms. Conway. This is Gladys at Discreet Talent Connections. I am calling to inform you that you have been selected for a nanny position. The client has requested that you start immediately."

I frowned. "Nanny? I thought I would be assigned an assistant or an office job."

There was a sigh. "Ms. Conway." The irritation in Gladys's voice transmitted across the phone. "We provide a variety of talent to our clients. Whatever needs they express, we find a way to meet and exceed them. Your information stated that you have experience with young children. Is that not the case? If there is a problem or any doubt about your ability to perform, then we can remove your file from our roster."

"No, there's no problem! I mean, I'm just surprised at the assignment. It's so sudden. When and where do you need me?" I hadn't lied in my interview. Not exactly. I only omitted the part where my experience was babysitting my seven-year-old cousin during family get-togethers on Thanksgivings and Christmases.

"The client, Mr. Wulfthorn has requested your presence at Wulfthorn Baked Goods Corporation for an initial interview. You will be caring for a four-year-old girl, Emilia Wulfthorn. She's very well-behaved, but her guardian needs someone to look after her while he is at work. The term of the contract is for one year, and you will receive compensation of one hundred thousand dollars."

I stared wide-eyed at Katie in shock at the amount. Wow, she mouthed silently.

"Ms. Conway, I must warn you, Mr. Wulfthorn is one of our most demanding clients. If you want the job, you will need to be at his office by 2 PM on the dot. Will this be a problem?"

Katie picked up her phone and flashed the screen at me. Shit. It was already 12:30. How was I going to clean up and get there in time? Katie nodded her head frantically.

"Take it," she whispered.

"I'll be there," I blurted.

"Excellent. If your interview goes well today, I will send you the contract and documents to be signed. Best of luck, Ms. Conway."

I stared at the phone in shock as the call ended.

My eyes met Katie's. "Holy shit!" we shouted.

She wrapped her arms around me, and we jumped in excitement. "I can't believe you got a job!"

"Well, it's not a job yet, unless I can get across town at the speed of light," I said.

"Go," Katie ordered. She grabbed me by the shoulders and

pushed me in the direction of the bathroom. "I'll find something for you to wear. You get cleaned up."

"I need shoes too!" I shouted. Thankfully, the two of us shared the same size.

Katie was already rummaging through her closet by the time I stripped out of my clothes. I wet a washcloth and swabbed my chest where most of the coffee had landed and soaked through my shirt.

She came into the bathroom and shoved a chunky dark gray knit sweater and light gray pants in my direction. On the floor, she placed a pair of tawny-colored loafers. "It's not the latest in fashion, but it's professional. You know how these corporate places can be."

I shrugged on the clothes and while I got dressed, Katie tapped away at her phone. "Wow, listen to this."

"I'm listening," I grunted as I pulled the sweater over my head.

"Your boss is the youngest founder of a food empire worth over ten billion dollars. He started his first bakery in Huntington Harbor at the age of twenty-two and by the time he was twenty-nine, expanded his chain of bakeries to over thirty countries."

As she filled me in on the guy I was going to be working for, I finger combed my hair into a somewhat presentable state. Frizzy strands stood up in a halo around my head, but that was unavoidable with all the humidity from the rain. I pushed my glasses back up my nose with my finger.

"I wonder what he looks like?" Katie scrolled on her phone and frowned. "Strange. I can't find a single picture of this dude. Shit, you've got to go. It's 12:45 already. The next bus is at 12:50."

"Fuck!" I ran out to the living room to grab my phone and keys before flying out the door.

"Good luck. Try not to sleep with your billionaire boss on the first day," Katie's voice called out as I ran down the street to the bus stop.

As if that was ever going to happen.

CHAPTER 2

BLAKE

"Not now!" I snarled. As soon as the elevator doors opened, my assistant, Anna, jumped to her feet. She rushed to the other side of her desk as soon as she saw me. The entire top floor was my executive suite consisting of a waiting room, meeting room, and my own private office. I stormed through the waiting room, brushed past Anna on my way to my office, and slammed the door behind me.

A part of me winced at how much of an asshole I was to her, but it didn't matter. Putting up with me was part of her job, and she was compensated handsomely for it.

"What the fuck happened to you, dude?" Reeve Song, my best friend and lifelong business partner looked at me from where he stood at the giant window overlooking the city below. Reeve was like a brother to me, and we were part of the same wolf pack. If any other person intruded on my personal domain like this, I would have ripped their head off. He was the only person in the world I trusted besides my kin.

He scanned me up and down, pausing at the giant coffee stain on my shirt. "Did you dump your breakfast all over yourself?"

Tugging at my tie, I practically shredded my suit jacket and shirt with my claws as I ripped them off. "A hazard of on-site recon," I replied. I strode to the other side of the room where I kept several fresh sets of suits in my office closet.

"What are you doing here? Don't you have to give a speech at the RIDTech conference right now?" I asked. Reeve was a pioneer of online retail and his expertise was what allowed Wulfthorn Baked Goods to dominate the home bread delivery market.

Once I was out of the soiled clothes, and no longer smelling like a walking coffee cart, my heartbeat slowed. Like the hazy fog outside, my temper faded away under the bright light of day.

Reeve gave a long sigh that I heard even from across the room. "Petra quit."

I stuck my head out of the closet. "Again?" Petra was Reeve's assistant, also known as his walking brain and calendar.

Reeve nodded. "For real this time and without a word. Her resignation letter was on her desk this morning. I was jet-lagged from flying back from London and dealing with Dad's estate. The conference totally slipped from my mind."

I tugged the knot of my tie into place. "How many times have I told you not to be such a jerk to her? It was bound to bite you in the ass eventually."

Reeve scoffed. He jerked his head in the direction of my office door, where Anna was sitting on the other side. "Dude, you're one to talk. Pot meet kettle."

I joined Reeve at the window. Together, we looked down at the bustling street fifty stories below us. Up here, among the clouds, the people below looked like little ants crawling around my feet. We may as well have been gods watching the world from the heavens. It was lonely at the top, but this was what I had pursued my entire life.

"Fisher's ready to make a move," Reeve said.

Fisher was the founder of the Bean Brewing and Sipping coffee shops. For over two months, I had been trying to work out a deal to buy his company. He was going to retire soon. After devoting his entire life to expanding the reach of his company, it was well deserved. From one tiny coffee shop in Huntington Harbor, he expanded his company until every city in every state in the country had a Bean Brewing coffee shop. Too bad he didn't have an heir to take over the company after he stepped down. Still, the old goat refused to sell to me. Not that I was going to give him a choice. That company was going to be mine eventually.

My goal this morning was to analyze the staff and operating procedures at the coffee shop. I wanted to spot any inefficiencies that could be improved upon and examine the way the employees interacted with their customers. My entire empire was built upon a neurotic attention to detail and a willingness to take down anyone who dared to stand in my way.

Owning a nationwide chain of coffee shops where I could also sell products from my own company was the next step in expanding my empire. I wanted to see Wulfthorn's pastries and breads in every coffee shop and every store in this country and the world. Bean Brewing and Sipping was a vital step in that plan.

"Is it Unibrod?" I asked.

Reeve put his hands in his pants pockets and gave a nonchalant shrug. "Most likely. My sources found out that Fisher's meeting someone in Paradise Peaks after the new year. Now we know why he's been dicking you along."

I wasn't the only one who had my eye on Fisher's coffee business. Unibrod, the world's biggest conglomerate of fast food brands, wanted to gobble up Bean Brewing and add it to their portfolio. The very thought insulted me to my core. Like my own bakeries, Fisher ran his business with passion and the utmost attention to the quality of his products. I was going to fight to my last tooth to get this company and keep it from becoming another stale chain that sold overpriced burned coffee.

"I need to beat them to Fisher. Make him an offer he can't refuse. No matter what, I'm going to close this deal," my words were almost a growl as they came out.

Victory was so close. There was no way I was going to let this opportunity slip out of my grasp. Whether Fisher knew it or not, I had my sights locked on him. The wolf inside of me was not going to let up the hunt until I captured my prey.

Reeve sat down in my leather chair and picked up the tiny rake next to the Zen sand garden on my desk. He raked a circle around the bonsai tree in the center. "Better get on it. Fisher's going to spend the entire month of December in Paradise Peaks. It'll be the perfect time to ambush him. Unibrod already has their lackeys swarming all over." He stacked a pebble on top of another. "No more time for runs to the coffee shop."

I sighed at the reminder of what happened this morning. What was supposed to be a quick data-gathering visit turned into a nightmare because of some clumsy woman who looked like she just got off the bus from bumfuck somewhere.

Not that it was a bad thing. She had an intriguing openness about her that was missing in the jaded cosmopolitan women who stalked the streets of Huntington Harbor in their stiletto heels.

The time we had together was brief, but the moment I touched her, it felt right. Perfectly right in a way I never experienced before. Her soft body molded to mine when she bumped into me, and she wasn't a chore to look at. Not at all. Behind her heavy dark-rimmed glasses, she had thick long lashes and sharp brown eyes. Though the rain turned her hair into a frizzy puff, her soft brown locks fell past her shoulders in a wavy waterfall that I ached to sink my fingers into. Even through all the layers she wore, it was clear she had the right amount of curves in all the right places.

Despite her awkwardness and the power difference between us, she had a silent confidence about her. Not many people dared hold their heads up high and glare at me the way she did, especially after she spilled her drink all over me.

Then there was her scent. It was difficult to describe. Sweet and musky, with a lingering trace of honeysuckle and fresh fall apples. I took a deep breath through my nose as if I could conjure up her aroma through memory. She smelled like home in some unseen paradise I had never been to.

Something about this woman stirred a part of me that I did not wish to confront. It was something primal and overwhelming. Unable to face her any longer without losing control, I did what an alpha wolf never did. I ran out of the coffee shop with my tail between my legs.

A high-pitched childish giggle pierced the silence of my office before the door burst open. "Uncle Blake! Up!"

Emilia, my niece, dashed toward me with the frenetic speed and agility that only wolf pups possessed. She wore purple leggings under a black tutu covered with glitter that twinkled in the light, and a pink t-shirt decorated with a rabbit jumping over a rainbow. In one of her hands, she clutched a ragged stuffed bunny that flailed its limbs as she flung it around. Poor Mr. Snuffle's head lolled back, and its beady black eyes gleamed up at me as if it wanted to exit this plane of existence.

I held out my arms and hefted her up as she crashed into me in a whirlwind of gangly legs and grabby hands. Wrapping her little arms around my neck, she watched with gleaming mischievous eyes as my assistant scrambled clumsily after her.

"Mr. Wulfthorn," Anna gasped. She was winded and out of breath from chasing after the child. Messy strands of blonde hair streaked with silver escaped from her normally neat French twist. "I'm terribly sorry. She got away from me. It won't happen again."

"It's alright, Anna," I assured her. It wasn't really, though. Emilia could have gotten hurt. She was the only remaining link I had to my late sister, and as the heir to the Wulfthorn empire, she had to be protected. Still, Reeve's predicament echoed in the back of my mind. As much as this current situation was chaos, it would be even more of a mess if Anna quit on me. "No harm done. The child is safe. Why don't you take an early lunch break."

She started to protest.

Holding up a hand, I interrupted her. "I insist on it. Emilia and I have a lot to catch up on. There are important matters of tea parties with Mr. Snuffles to discuss."

My niece let out a playful giggle.

"Send an order down to the kitchen for Emilia's lunch to be delivered to my office."

"Yes, sir. The usual, sir?"

I nodded. Though we had lived together for less than a month, Emilia was like me, a Wulfthorn through and through. We knew what we liked, and exactly how we liked it. The only difference was, I didn't throw a tantrum before every meal.

"Want anything, Reeve?" I asked.

He shook his head. "I'm not hungry. Thank you, Anna."

Anna exited the room, closing the door behind her.

"Did you have a good nap?" I asked Emilia.

She wrinkled her nose and squirmed. I bent down and let her slip out of my arms.

"No. Anna smells like stinky medicine. I don't like it here." She stuck out her little lip and pouted before she stomped over to my desk. Climbing onto my chair, she dragged Mr. Snuffles onto my desk and began to rearrange the rocks in my Zen garden.

I sighed. In the short time since my sister's death and discovering that I was now Emilia's only living family member, I still did not have anybody who I trusted to watch my niece while I was at the office.

Reeve chuckled. "She has a point. This has to be the most expensive daycare in Huntington Harbor. The office is no place for a kid. There's nothing for her to do and nobody around to play with her except for us old farts. Not to mention, you have to figure out the acquisition. How are you going to poach Fisher ahead of Unibrod and babysit at the same time?"

"I'll figure something out," I grumbled. He was right. As much as I loved Emilia, this was the last thing I needed at the moment. The current situation was untenable. I could concentrate on work, or on family, but not both at the same time.

At that moment, the phone outside my office rang. Normally, I would have let the call go to voicemail until Anna came back to deal with it, but something inside of me pushed me to go out and answer it.

I picked up the phone. "Blake Wulfthorn."

"Good afternoon, Mr. Wulfthorn, this is Gladys at Discreet Talent Connections. I am happy to inform you that we have found a nanny who meets all the criteria you provided."

I grunted. "Did you do a full background check on her?"

"Certainly. Her name is Lacey Conway, twenty-three years old. She passed with flying colors, not so much as a parking ticket. Graduated summa cum laude and has experience babysitting young children, as well as glowing recommendations from her previous employers."

"Send her over to my office ASAP today. I want her to start immediately."

"I will make arrangements right away. If there are any further concerns, please feel free to contact the agency."

Once I ended the call, I sent a request to my security team to run a background check on her. Not that I didn't trust the employment agency, but there was no such thing as being too careful when it came to my family.

Surprise and shock made me freeze when I opened the door to my office. Reeve was on all fours, with two pieces of tissue paper taped to his forehead. The tissue was twisted so it stood upright out of his head. Emilia sat on his back, her little hands clutching at the nape of his shirt.

"Faster, bunny! We have to make it to the other side before the wolf gets us."

I closed the door behind me and crossed my arms. "What is going on here?"

Emilia laughed. "Uncle Reeve is a giant bunny!"

Gently, I lifted her off his back. "I can see that. You're looking particularly bright-eyed and bushy-tailed, Reeve. It's a good look on you."

Reeve rose to his feet and flexed his neck and back. He waited until Emilia ran across the room to the window. Once she was distracted, he held up his middle finger and made an obscene motion at me.

"The kid looked like she was going to cry," he grumbled. "It was the only thing I could think of to make her stop. Swear on our pack that what you saw will never leave this room."

I chuckled. "Your secret is safe with me. I swear." I gestured at his head. "Those may raise questions among the office staff."

He scowled and ripped off the pieces of tissue stuck to his head. "I thought you were going to get a nanny to take care of the kid." Tossing the paper into the wastebasket, he moved to the mini-bar and began fixing himself a drink.

"I did, and I have. That was the employment agency on the phone. They're sending someone over this afternoon." Leaning my hip against the edge of my desk, I looked at Emilia who was describing the happenings on the street below to Mr. Snuffles. "The help can't come soon enough."

Reeve sat on one of the seats facing my desk. The ice clinked against his glass as he brought the tumbler up to his lips. "That was fast. Maybe I should have them find me an assistant." He swallowed. "That is if your new nanny doesn't run out of here screaming by the end of the day."

His phone buzzed in his pocket. Reeve finished his drink and got up. "As fun as this visit was, I've got to get back to my office before the interns set the place on fire."

A discreet knock on the door interrupted our conversation.

"Come in," I called out.

The door opened and revealed Sammy, the head chef at Balsamic, the upscale Italian restaurant in my office building, and also my personal chef at the office. He pushed a serving cart containing Emilia's lunch.

"Thank you, Sammy. Just place the food on my desk."

Reeve slipped past him out of room.

"Right away, sir." Sammy moved with the speed and efficiency of someone who had worked in a professional kitchen for years. In fact, I had poached the young sous chef from one of my favorite restaurants in the city. The head chef he worked under kept him on a tight leash, refusing to let Sammy develop his own skills or have any input on the dishes in his kitchen. Now that Sammy ran his own kitchen, he had full creative control, except of course, when it came to my niece's orders.

Sammy placed a place mat on the desk, then a complete place setting with kid-sized silverware and cloth napkin. Finally, he set a plate in the center. He removed the silver bell cover and revealed the same meal that Emilia ate every afternoon. Chicken nuggets and a side of matchstick carrots with ketchup and ranch dressing on the side. Next to the plate, he placed a small cup of milk.

From the lower compartment of the serving cart, he pulled out a booster seat and placed it on my chair. With a quick bow, Sammy excused himself and exited the room.

"Time for lunch, Emilia."

Silently, I let out a sigh of relief when she came over without protest. Ever since she came to live with me, meal times had been a daily struggle. I lifted her up into her booster seat and pushed the chair into place.

She examined the plate silently. Her face flushed, in the all too familiar sign of an impending tantrum.

"Emilia..."

Her face scrunched up, and she let out an ear-piercing screech. She kicked her legs and thrashed her arms. "No! It's wrong. All wrong." Emilia scrambled out of her booster seat and ran to hide behind the chair where Reeve had been sitting.

In the midst of the chaos, my office door popped open. It was Anna. She stuck her head in and looked at the scene with a horrified expression on her face.

"What now?" I snarled.

"Mr. Wulfthorn, your nanny is here," she announced.

The door opened all the way and someone I had thought I would never see again stepped in.

Though she no longer looked like a drowned cat, she stared at me in wide-eyed silence, as if she had seen a ghost.

A grin tugged at my lips. "Hello, Oklahoma."

CHAPTER 3

LACEY

It was him. No way. Standing right in front of me was the guy at the coffee shop who was last seen wearing my flat white coffee on his chest.

"What's wrong? Cat got your tongue?" He smirked. The corners of his lips quirked as if he found the situation amusing.

I blinked. "This has to be some kind of mistake. I'm looking for a Mr. Wulfthorn. I'm his new nanny."

"There's no mistake, Oklahoma."

My hands squeezed until my nails dug into my palms. "My name is Lacey," I said through gritted teeth. How I wanted to slap that smug look off his face, but that wasn't exactly the way to endear oneself to one's new boss.

"Lacey, then. Your interview begins right now. Your first task is to get Emilia to eat her lunch." He gestured for me to step further into his office.

For the first time, I took in the room. Framed by a row of floor-to-ceiling windows behind a massive glass desk, the office overlooked the busy streets of Huntington Harbor below. Sunlight flooded the room, highlighting how perfect and sterile it was. Everything was dark leather, glass, and polished metal. It was masculine, cold, and expensive. Definitely not the place for a four-year-old child.

The child turned out to be an adorable girl with big round hazel eyes. Her shiny black hair was tied in a messy ponytail. Sitting on the floor, she clutched a stuffed rabbit in her arms as she sulked behind a black leather chair with metal legs.

With a quiet snick, the door closed behind me. I was all alone with the fearsome Mr. Wulfthorn and my new charge.

Emilia stared up at me with wary reserve.

What had happened to her to make her so distrustful at such a young age? Maybe this would work better if I got on her level. Carefully, I kneeled next to her.

"Hi, Emilia. My name is Lacey. And who is your friend here?"

She fiddled with the stuffed toy's ear in between her fingers. "Mr. Snuffles."

"Mr. Snuffles looks like he's hungry."

Emilia sniffed. "I'm hungry too."

"Okay, then let's get you something to eat. Can you get up?"

She shook her head.

With a pleading glance at Mr. Wulfthorn, I gestured my head in the direction of the food I noticed on his desk. His expression was closed off and unreadable, and for a moment, I was afraid he wasn't going to help me.

He nodded. Moving with a quick confident stride, he retrieved the entire place setting and brought it over to me. I took the plate and examined the contents. It seemed like all four-year-olds had the same tastebuds, even if they had a billionaire at their beck and call.

I placed the plate on the floor in front of Emilia, then the cup of milk and the silverware. At the sight of the food, she scrunched up her face and turned her head away. Even as inexperienced with children as I was, I spotted the impending meltdown.

Nervously, I nudged my glasses up my nose. "What's wrong, Emilia?"

She clutched the stuffed toy to her chest and shook her head.

Well, this wasn't going very well. There was no need to turn around to know that Mr. Wulftorn was not impressed with my childcare skills. I was totally failing this interview.

Wait a minute. My eyes landed on the stuffed rabbit and then the cartoon rabbit on her shirt. An idea struck me.

First, I used a fork to arrange all the chicken nuggets in a circle on the plate. Then, I split a matchstick carrot in half and placed the pieces above a nugget, so that they formed a pair of bunny ears. I repeated this until every nugget had a set of ears.

By now, both Wulfthorns were staring at what I was doing with fascination.

"Do you like ketchup or ranch, Emilia?" I asked gently.

"Both." She climbed to her hands and knees and crept closer to me. Her eyes lit up as she watched me work.

"A lady of refined tastes," I commented. Using the spoon, I

placed big dollops of ranch dressing on each nugget, giving them fluffy cotton tails. Finally, I drew ketchup eyes and whiskers on the nuggets.

"Bunnies!" Emilia whispered in amazement. "I used to have blueberry bunny pancakes with Mommy."

I set the fork down on the plate. My heart broke at the sadness in her voice as she mentioned her mother.

"I'm sure they were the best pancakes, sweetheart."

A muscle in Mr. Wulfthorn's jaw jumped. "We can have bunny pancakes too. I'll tell Chef Rosa to make some tomorrow morning if that's what you like."

The solemn expression on Emilia's face finally broke, stretching into a smile. "Okay, Uncle Blake." She glanced over at me. "Can I eat the bunnies now, Lacey?"

"Of course, Emilia. They're all for you."

She scooched closer to the plate and picked up the fork. Spearing a nugget, she brought it up to her mouth and took a big bite. After chewing for a while, she grinned and murmured her approval.

She ate happily, tackling each bunny in the same order, body first, then the ears.

Together, Mr. Wulfthorn and I watched her eat her lunch without complaint.

"Impressive," he commented. "You did well, Okla--Lacey."

"Does that mean I've got the job, Mr. Wulfthorn?" I couldn't help but beam on the inside.

"Blake, please. Mr. Wulfthorn makes me feel like my father."

"So, what's the verdict, Blake?"

"You're skilled at getting her to eat, but I still have some concerns."

I gaped at him. "I just pulled off a miracle here."

"True, but your clumsiness makes me doubt your ability to keep Emilia out of harm's way."

Heat flushed up my neck and face as I recalled the incident in the coffee shop. That wasn't even my fault. The indignation burned, that he was holding the accident he caused against me.

"Not that you're to blame, there was no way for you to know I was standing behind you," he muttered.

I swallowed the triumph that bubbled in my throat. This was as much of an apology as I was ever going to get from a proud man like him.

The sun shining through the windows lit up his features. My breath caught at the long angular lines of his face. At that moment, he resembled a masterfully chiseled sculpture.

Blake studied his niece as she munched happily through her lunch. She made each of the nugget bunnies hop across the plate and then up to Mr. Snuffle's mouth before bringing each nugget up to her mouth.

Despite his closed-off demeanor, I could tell that he really did care for the little girl.

"This is the calmest mealtime we've had since she moved in with me." A frown formed on his face. "I'm not promising to hire you yet, but I'm willing to give you a chance."

I rose to my feet, even though I would never be tall enough to stand neck to neck with Blake. This was still a business negotiation, and I needed to be on firm footing. "What are you proposing?"

"I have an operations meeting with my staff downstairs for the remainder of the afternoon. If the kid is still alive when I come back from my meeting, then you've got the job."

I blinked. That was it? How hard could it be to keep my eyes on one little girl? "You've got yourself a deal."

Holding out my hand, I waited until he grasped mine in a firm handshake. To my surprise, his hand fit around mine perfectly. I had to fight back the sigh of disappointment when he finally let go.

Blake cleared his throat. "Emilia has a temporary play area set up in the waiting room. You can stay with her there while I'm gone." He let out a breath. "I'm trusting you with the most important person in my life. Do you have a handle on this?"

Did I? I didn't know if I could handle myself most days. Squaring my chin, I gave him a firm nod. "I will do everything to make sure she is taken care of. I promise."

"I'm sure you'll do your very best. If you need anything, ask Anna." He paused. "She looks innocent, but this one will try to bend you to her will. Be careful."

I glanced down at the little girl who had eaten all of her nuggets and was finishing up the last of her carrot sticks. Every drop of milk in her cup was gone. She beamed up at me, giving me a dimpled smile. How could that be true? Emilia was as sweet and cute as the bunnies she loved so much.

"You have your job, and I have mine. Please trust that I can do what you hired me to do."

"Very well." His tone was mild, like the skilled business negotiator he was. He revealed nothing of his true thoughts.

"Come on, Emilia," I called out. "I heard that you have a play area. Can you show me where it is?"

The child scrambled to her feet, dragging her stuffed animal by the arm. She crashed into my side and crooked her finger, beckoning me toward her. I leaned down to hear what she had to say.

"You have to find me first," she whispered. Then, before I could figure out what she meant, she ran to the office door and dashed out into the waiting room. Maybe I was getting old, but never in my life had I seen a child run that fast.

Blake chuckled. "Told you. She's a master at hide and seek."

I exited Blake's office and began the search for my charge. It was fifteen minutes before I found her tucked away in one of the shelves under the counter of the coffee bar. She was hiding behind stacks of paper cups, stir sticks, and bottles of syrup.

"You got off easy, little wolf children will test you to see if you are worthy of respect," Anna said, all while keeping her eyes on her computer monitor. Her fingers danced across the keyboard in a rhythmic tap tap tap as she spoke. "The last time she made me find her, she somehow pried open the metal grating and hid in the air duct. I was moments away from calling the police to report a missing child."

Ah, that explained everything. I had a sense that there was something supernatural about the Wulfthorns. They were wolf shifters. Before I came here, I was aware that their kind inhabited Huntington Harbor, but I had no idea that I would become familiar with an actual shifter family so soon, and so intimately.

Emilia giggled as she climbed out of the coffee bar. "That was fun, Lacey. Let's play again."

No, not again. Never again, if I could help it. "Can you show me your play area? Your Uncle Blake says it's pretty awesome."

"Uh huh. Uncle Blake took me to the store. We got lots of toys!"

"I can see that," I said.

Emilia led me over to what she called Bunnyville, a make-believe town inhabited completely by bunnies. It had a play kitchen that served as a diner,

a grocery store with a cash register, and even a functioning miniature pink car that served as the town's public transit system. It seemed like whatever time he couldn't give to his niece, he replaced with toys.

We spent the rest of the afternoon playing pretend mayor of Bunnyville. By the time Blake came back from his meeting, Emilia was fast asleep on the couch in the waiting area under a soft chenille throw. Anna had ended her shift over an hour ago and left us alone.

Blake rushed out of the elevator, but before he could say a word, I held my finger up to my lips and shushed him, gesturing toward his sleeping niece with my head.

"I'm sorry, the meeting went longer than I anticipated. How was she?" His expression was contrite and marred with lines of stress. He was being pulled in multiple directions. No matter how rich he was, he couldn't do it all alone.

"Like an angel."

He tutted. "You're a terrible liar. Tell the truth, what did she do?"

"I did think I lost her for a moment, but I found her hiding spot in the end."

"She's been doing that a lot lately, hiding away. It's been a recurring theme ever since her mother passed away." Blake cleared his throat. "You did well today, Lacey. I'm impressed. The paperwork still needs to be finalized, but you're hired."

"Oh, wow. Really?" I couldn't believe it. I just told him I thought I lost his niece and he was still going to give me the job.

He rolled his eyes. "I wouldn't say it if I didn't mean it."

"Of course. I can start whenever you need me." My nerves made my voice shake as reality started sinking in. This job was going to set me up financially for the rest of my life.

"That's what I like to hear. From now on, my driver will pick you up at your place at 5:30 every morning."

My eyes widened. "How do you know where I live?"

"Do you think I wouldn't run my own background check on you? I know everything about you, including where you've lived your entire life, to that allergic reaction you had to corn when you were twelve, as well as your non-existent experience with childcare." His eyes pierced me. It was like he could see into the depths of my soul.

My face flushed with heat as he revealed my deepest secrets.

Of course, my new boss was ruthless. He didn't become a billionaire in such a short time by overlooking any details.

"But Emilia likes you, which I can't say about many people in this world." He pinned me with hard eyes. "5:30 sharp tomorrow. Be ready."

CHAPTER 4

BLAKE

The next morning, I supervised as Chef Rosa, my private chef at home, made bunny pancakes. The kitchen already smelled heavenly of crispy fried bacon and scrambled eggs which sat under the warmer.

Despite my better judgment, I went to the espresso machine and prepared another cup. As I waited for the coffee to drip out, I glanced down at my watch. It was almost seven o'clock. My driver would be here with Lacey at any moment.

Over at the kitchen island, Emilia was busy having a tea party with Mr. Snuffles. The tea was actually water, and the cups were plastic, but the bunny shaped cinnamon raisin buns were baked fresh by my own hands last night. Whenever I was plagued with insomnia, I resorted to the one thing I did best. I baked. There was nothing quite as effective as kneading out my frustrations into a ball of dough.

Thoughts of Lacey swam around my brain, keeping me tossing restlessly for hours. It was as if she was right there in my bedroom. Despite all my efforts to push her away, my blood pulsed with the anticipation of seeing her and getting to know her better.

The last drops of coffee dripped out, and like a possessed creature, I reached for the cup. There was no need for milk or sugar today. Pure unadulterated caffeine was what I wanted flowing through my veins.

I wondered if I had been hasty in hiring Lacey.

Her qualifications for the nanny position were sparse, to say the least. Had I been thinking with my dick instead of my head?

The employment contract was signed by both parties and finalized by email last night. As her employer, I had almost all the power in the relationship. If it turned out that she really couldn't handle the job, I could just fire her and pay a ten percent penalty clause. Considering that I had shoes that cost more than that, it wasn't even a slap on the wrist.

Not that I expected to fire her any time soon. Not when she blushed so fetchingly whenever I provoked her. Dirty thoughts flooded my mind. What other unspeakable things could I do to make her cheeks flush like that? Would she bite her lips and beg for more when I pounded my dick into her and drove her to ecstasy?

I shook my head. No. There was going to be no touching of the pretty little nanny. Even if she smelled delicious and had the most perfect bouncy tits that she kept hidden under that ugly sweater she wore yesterday.

"I don't want them!" Emilia shouted.

I turned around to find my chef and my niece glaring at each other over a plate of steaming pancakes. Chef Rosa had a spatula in one hand pointed at the child and her other hand on her hip, while Emilia sulked with her arms crossed over her chest. Neither of them showed any sign of backing down from the standoff.

Rosa pointed the spatula threateningly at me. "This goes beyond the scope of my employment contract. I cook. I clean. I keep the kitchen stocked. I do not babysit." She tossed the spatula into the sink, turned off the stove, and stormed out of the kitchen.

I let out a long sigh. At this rate, I was going to lose all of my staff at home and at work if I didn't get a handle on this situation. "Fucking great," I muttered.

A sniffle cut through my frustration like a knife. Emilia looked like she was on the verge of tears. "I'm sorry, Uncle Blake," she said through her hiccups.

My heart plummeted to my stomach. "Oh, Emilia, there's nothing to be sorry for. You haven't done anything wrong." I brushed her hair out of her face. "I'm very new at this, and I'm sure you miss your mommy very much."

She nodded.

"I miss her too," I said softly.

Emilia threw her arms around my torso. "Don't leave, Uncle Blake. Not like Mommy."

I looked down at her in surprise. "Oh, sweetheart. I promise never to leave you." Something sharp pierced my stone-code heart, cracking it open. It was the truth. I would die for her and destroy anyone who dared harm a hair on her head.

My ears twitched. Vaguely, I heard voices and footsteps

coming from the garage door. Even before I saw her, I knew it was Lacey.

Rosa came back, bringing Lacey with her. My chef nodded curtly at me before disappearing.

Lacey paused in the doorway and took in the scene, as if uncertain of the situation she had walked into.

"Lacey!" Emilia cried out. She kicked her feet against the booster seat.

"Good morning, Emilia." Lacey walked over to the island and hung the strap of her purse on the back of one of the chairs. "Good morning, Blake." She examined the two of us with curious eyes.

"Morning, Lacey." I swigged the last of my coffee. "We're having breakfast difficulties."

Lacey glanced at Emilia's untouched plate. "I see," she said.

I mumbled an excuse to deposit the dirty cup in the sink. From there, I watched silently as she leaned against the counter next to Emilia.

Leaning down until she was at Emilia's level, Lacey spoke to her in a low soft voice. "These pancakes look delicious. Are they bunnies?"

Emilia shook her head.

"No? What's wrong with them?"

"That's not how Mommy makes them."

"Oh. Why don't you tell me how to make them, then?"

"It needs to be sweet and fluffy," Emilia said. "Woosh!"

Lacey glanced over at me and shared a look.

"Do you mean whipped cream?" I asked. Of course. It all made sense. I went over to the fridge and pulled out a can of whipped cream.

My niece's eyes lit up and she clapped. "Yeah!"

"Okay, Emilia. Show me how you want it." Holding the can upside down in position, I let her little hands guide me. We squirted the sweet topping onto the pancake until the entire thing was covered under a mound of fluffy whiteness. I had my doubts that my sister let her child eat this much sugar for breakfast, but if this was what it took for Emilia to eat her breakfast, then so be it.

"And eyes," she demanded imperially like the little dictator she was.

Lacey spotted the bowl of blueberries by the stove and brought them over. She let Emilia do the honors of adding two blueberries to the pile of cream.

Finally satisfied that the pancakes were to her standards, Emilia picked up a fork and dug into her breakfast.

My phone buzzed on the counter. Picking it up, I scrolled through the message. It was Anna, informing me that I was late for my meeting. I pocketed my phone and picked up the rest of my things. "Be good for Lacey, okay?"

"Yes, Uncle Blake." To my surprise, Emilia didn't even look up from her pancakes.

"Go on, I've got it from here," Lacey reassured me. "If I need anything, I'll ask Rosa."

Despite my doubts about her abilities, she had handled Emilia's tantrum with flying colors. She was good at her job. Really good.

The day at the office dragged on. For the first time in my life, I didn't care about new products our research department created, or how much market share we gained in the Chinese market. As I listened to my employees talk about sales figures and customer value, all I wanted to do was go home and eat pancakes with my girls.

By the time I came back home, Emilia was already tucked in bed, and Lacey sat in a chair next to her bed reading a bedtime story to her.

I watched them from the doorway as Lacey finished the story. Emilia blinked sleepily, giving me a little wave with her fingers before she clutched Mr. Snuffles close to her chest and snuggled into her covers. Lacey put her finger up to her lips and turned off the light, leaving a single nightlight on before stepping out into the hallway.

Together, we made our way downstairs and toward the kitchen.

"How was she?" I asked.

"I could say that she was an angel, but then I would be a liar," she said with a grin.

I let out a chuckle.

We walked into an empty kitchen. It was late and Rosa was already off duty. I went to the fridge and pulled out a beer. I offered Lacey one. She shook her head.

"Are you sure? If you don't trust my driver to take you home, I can do it."

"Oh, it's not that." She paused for a moment, as if unsure if she should say more. "I plan on getting some writing done when I get home."

I raised my eyebrows. This was interesting. My nanny was full of surprises. "What's your book going to be about?"

"It's a paranormal romance novel about vampires with mind-reading powers. I know it sounds cheesy."

I shook my head. "No, it's an intriguing premise. A romance novel published at the right time riding the market trends can become a major hit." I gestured at the espresso machine. "What about a coffee, then?"

Lacey gazed longingly at it. "Black coffee sounds wonderful. I wanted to make one during the day, but I didn't want to break the machine."

"You're free to use anything you need while you're here." I gestured for her to come closer. "Come on, I'll show you how to use this thing. It's not hard."

She moved close enough that I could smell her delicious scent. I swallowed hard. It took all of my focus to keep my hands steady as I showed her how to tamp the coffee grounds and start the machine. Even though she didn't want any milk in her coffee tonight, I demonstrated how to use the frother. Covering her hand with mine, we moved the container of milk around until it was filled with the perfect amount of foam.

"Huh, that wasn't as complicated as I thought it would be."

I handed the cup of coffee to her and went to clean out the grounds. "I think writing a novel is far more difficult. That's a very impressive goal. I would love to read it when you're finished."

She nodded, hiding her smile behind her cup as she took a sip of coffee.

Over the next several weeks, we settled into a comfortable routine. Lacey would arrive in the mornings and the three of us would have breakfast together before I headed to work. After the first night, I rearranged my schedule so that I could get home early. We would have dinner like we were a family before Lacey would head home. Both Emilia and I were reluctant to see her go at the end of the day.

Under Lacey's care and a stable daily schedule at home, Emilia's tantrums over her food stopped.

One night, it was my turn to read Emilia her bedtime story while Lacey put away her clothes in the chest of drawers. As Emilia was curled up by my side, she asked the question I had been hesitant to voice out of fear of rejection.

"Is Lacey going to come with us for Christmas?"

Lacey shot me a curious look in the middle of folding a t-shirt. "What's this about?"

I cleared my throat. "I have to be in Paradise Peaks before and during the holidays for an important meeting. We'll be staying in a penthouse suite at the Hughes Hotel. Emilia and I would like it if you could come with us."

The shirt in her hands fell in a heap onto the drawer. "Oh, wow. I figured I would have the holidays off."

"If you already have plans, I can find other arrangements. You don't have to come if you don't want to." The disappointment settled in my stomach like bad coffee. Of course, she wasn't going to stay with us. The holidays were a time for family, real family, not the fake family she was paid to put up with.

"No, it's not that," Lacey blurted out. She picked up the crumpled shirt and folded it again. "I'm just surprised. My roommate already had plans to go home, so I was going to stay in and eat a gallon of caramel fudge ice cream all by myself while watching old reruns."

"What about your family?" Emilia asked with the innocence only a child could have.

Lacey pushed the drawer closed. She came to the bed and sat on the edge next to my legs. "My family lives very far away. Too far for me to go visit them this year," she said with a sad smile.

Emilia kicked off the covers and climbed onto her knees. She bounced with excitement. "You can have Christmas with me and Uncle Blake!"

Lacey shot me a glance. "I've never been to Paradise Peaks before. It's not exactly a world that I'm familiar with."

It finally dawned on me. She felt insecure about fitting into this new world. Her genuine nature was a refreshing change from the gold-digging vipers who usually clung to me. "Don't worry about anything. You'll be my guest. All of your expenses will be covered, I'll pay you overtime, and you'll stay in the penthouse with us. We'll fly in together on my plane. You can go explore all the tourist sites with Emilia while I'm working, and we can hit the ski slopes together. Think of it as a paid vacation."

"Okay, but only if I'm off the clock. All of this is already too much."

I sputtered. She was being ridiculous. How could I ask her to look after my niece for days for free? But the warning look in her eyes made me pause. She was serious.

"Alright. No overtime then."

"Then I accept your invitation."

Emilia shrieked with delight, climbing over my knees to get to Lacey. She threw her arms around her neck, and Lacey laughed as she picked her up in her arms.

I coughed to cover the strange flutter of nerves in my chest. Already, I pictured the three of us around a glittering tree on Christmas morning.

Even if I promised that I wouldn't pay her, that didn't mean that I couldn't make it up to her in other ways. My mind raced with ideas of what kind of presents I could get her.

I was going to make this a Christmas she was never going to forget.

CHAPTER 5

LACEY

Today started like every other morning. While Rosa was busy at the stove cooking up breakfast for all of us, I fixed Emilia's hair and kept her occupied with some kind of activity. Blake was in charge of making the coffee. Even though I now knew how to use the machine, coffee tasted better when it was brewed by him.

Not to mention the bread. As much as I adored Emilia, the fresh basket of flaky pain au chocolat or crusty sourdough was had a part in drawing me back to the Wulfthorn's house every morning. I had no idea how Blake managed to bake every morning with his busy schedule.

Today was casual Friday at the office, so he was wearing a dark maroon cashmere sweater and jeans. The outfit was simple and classic, but I knew that it cost thousands of dollars just by the quality of the fabric. He had his sleeves rolled up neatly. With each motion as he worked the machine, his forearms flexed and bunched making the wolf tattoo on his right arm wink as flesh and sinew rippled. Oh, how I wanted to stroke my hands up and down those muscles.

Emilia nudged my hand with her crayon, bringing me back to the task I was supposed to be paying attention to. I picked a pink crayon and colored a section of the unicorn bunny drawing.

But paying attention to the coloring page was a massive struggle. Blake dumped out the grounds and began tamping new grounds for the next cup of coffee. The sight of his strong tanned arms working was utterly distracting. Every one of his movements was graceful, but filled with power. Just like everything else about him.

Blake handed me my cappuccino and sat down next to me at the kitchen island. I brought the steaming hot cup to my face and inhaled the rich aroma. Closing my eyes, I took a sip. Absolute heaven. A happy moan of satisfaction escaped past my lips as the first bit of caffeine hit my blood.

When I opened my eyes, I found him staring at me. His eyes flicked down to my mouth.

Like a reflex, my tongue darted out to lick at the foam that clung to my top lip.

His nostrils flared and his lips parted. Hunger and impatience were etched on his face. Our breakfast being served cut through the tension in the air.

Chef Rosa shot both of us a knowing look as she brought over the rest of our breakfast. My cheeks heated. This was like the time in high school when my mother caught me making out with Danny on my front porch.

"Chocolate!" Emilia exclaimed.

Both Blake and I had a ham and cheese omelet, while Emilia had chocolate hazelnut crepes with strawberries. I helped Emilia cut her crepes into bite-sized pieces. She insisted that she was a big girl and that she and Mr. Snuffles could eat on their own.

Blake looked on with pride as Emilia ate without a fuss. She had come so far in the weeks I had known her. There was no trace of the anxious child she had been. Though I could never replace the mother she lost, I was honored and proud that I was a part of her healing journey.

As Blake and I dug into our food, I realized that we looked just like any other normal family having breakfast together. In moments like this, it was easy to forget why I was here. That I was paid to be here as his nanny. The thought pierced through my delusions. Getting attached to my boss could make everything into a complicated mess. I couldn't cross professional boundaries and risk losing this job, not only because of the money, but because Emilia needed me. I was his employee. Nothing more.

After Blake left for work, I spent a couple of hours playing with Emilia. During my first week, I got lost in the endless rooms of the house, but by now, I knew my way around like the back of my hand.

There were only two rules to playing hide and seek with Emilia. We had to stay in the family wing, and we couldn't go further into the garden area than the row of rosebushes. The servants' quarters were in the other wing of the house and Blake forbade Emilia or me from going into the forest surrounding the estate. He didn't state why, but it wasn't a big deal. Not that I wanted to go into the creepy dark woods, anyway.

Her attempts to outsmart me with her clever hiding spots were discovered in record time. After the excitement, we went to her playroom for craft time. Once she was tired out, it was time for her nap.

I wasn't going to let these rare moments of peace and quiet go wasted. As soon as Emilia was asleep, I gathered whatever notepads and scraps of paper I could find and wrote. While the final draft was going to be composed on my tablet, I liked working out the kinks in my idea by hand. Emilia usually slept for half an hour, which was plenty of time to get some words written and make actual progress toward finishing my novel. After her nap, she would play for another couple of hours before Blake came home from work, and we would have dinner together.

Days passed, and then it was time for us to go to Paradise Peaks. It was the night before we were going to fly out in the morning. Blake insisted I stay at his house for the first time since I began watching Emilia. My apartment was on the opposite side of Huntington Harbor, so it was easier for all three of us to be at the same place instead of having to rush across town to pick me up.

To my surprise, my room was right next to Emilia's room and one door down from Blake's bedroom. I had assumed that I would stay in the servant's wing.

After I packed her bags for the upcoming weeks away from home, Emilia begged to stay up and watch movies. The excitement of having her first sleepover was too much. Blake caved in to her request. The tough, stoic businessman was no match against his niece's sweet pleas.

We watched The Little Mermaid, with one of us on each side of Emilia. By the time the credits scrolled onto the screen, it was two hours past her bedtime. She was already snoring softly, with her head on a pillow on my lap.

"I'll put her to bed. You need to get some rest," Blake whispered. He bent over to scoop her into his arms, brushing against me as he did so. I wondered what it would be like to feel the muscles of his arms under my hand. The top two buttons of his shirt were unbuttoned, revealing the hair at the top of his chest. He smelled like coffee, pine trees, and his own irresistible musk.

Even as my heart thudded in my chest, I willed myself to breathe calmly and steadily. Silently, I prayed that he couldn't tell how much his touch affected me. I would never live down the embarrassment of being caught crushing on my boss. After all, I only worked for him. There was nothing going on between us.

I retreated to my room, but even through the walls that separated us, I could feel his presence, as keenly as if he was in the room with me. Closing my eyes, I tried to ignore him.

"Argh!" I kicked the covers off my overheated body and picked up my phone. There was a text message from Katie.

Katie: "Guess who got a job?"

I glanced at the time at the top of my phone. It wasn't even one o'clock yet, so she was probably still up. Quickly, I typed up a message.

Me: "Congrats! Is it with the agency?"

My phone dinged with the incoming reply. I knew my insomniac roommate would be the perfect distraction.

Katie: "Yep. My official title is Executive Assistant."

Me: "Sounds important. And a lot of work."

Katie: "Pssh. These jobs are 90% coffee runs and picking up dry cleaning. How hard could it be?"

Me: "Famous last words. When's your first day?"

Katie: "This week. I hope he's not a boss from hell and lets me go home for the holidays."

There was a pause.

Katie: "Not that I mean your boss is an a-hole."

Me: "It's fine. I have nowhere else to be anyway. Besides, the kid's cute."

Katie: "And Mr. Wulfthorn? Is he cute too?"

Me: "You have brain rot from all those smutty books you read about online. Shut up and go to bed."

Katie: "Ha. He is cute, I knew it. Luv you too!"

Eventually, I fell asleep with my phone in my hand. The next time I opened my eyes, it was already morning. Soft morning light sneaked in through the curtains. I checked my phone for the time. It was a little past five in the morning. Since my alarm was already set to go off in half an hour, I got out of bed and padded over to the ensuite bathroom.

After I finished my morning routine, I packed everything I was going to need for the next couple of weeks at Paradise Peaks into my luggage and went to wake Emilia.

I woke her with a gentle shake on the shoulder. "Good morning, sweetheart," I said softly.

Emilia blinked slowly. Her sleepy eyes lit up when she realized it was me.

"I dreamed you were here last night," she whispered.

I laughed. "No, I was really here. We had a sleepover and watched cartoons, remember?"

Despite being kept over her bedtime last night, Emilia did not put up a fuss over breakfast. As we ate, the driver took our bags out to the car.

Soon it was time to go. Blake was busy on his phone, so I grabbed Emilia's snow boots and jacket. "Are you excited to go on a plane today?" I asked as I helped her into her jacket.

She shook her head. "I used to fly to Uncle Blake's house with Mommy." After zipping up her jacket, I bent down to get her boots and secured the Velcro straps once she shoved her feet into them. Seeing that Emilia was dressed, I put on my own jacket and wrapped a thick knit scarf around my neck.

"Wow. That sounds like a lot of fun." I wasn't surprised that she had more air miles accumulated in her short four years on the planet than I had in my entire life. It was just one of the many reminders of how much more privileged the Wulfthorns were compared to my humble background.

We drove to the airport and all the way to the airstrip where Blake's private plane was waiting. From walking along the airstrip, to going up the stairs into the plane, the entire experience was surreal. The seats were all plush cream leather and arranged around a large polished wooden table. On the wall, there was a large television screen, and a door to what I assumed was the restroom.

We soon took off. I was mesmerized as I watched Huntington Harbor grow smaller and smaller beneath us from the window. The green fields and thick treetops soon turned into snow-capped mountain tops and sparse towering pine trees as we approached Paradise Peaks. There was already a limo waiting for us beside the airstrip when we landed.

As we drove up the winding mountain road, the pine trees along the side of the road grew taller and thicker, and then they were covered with a dusting of snow. The air grew cold and crisp with the chill of winter.

"Wow!"

Blake chuckled. "It's pretty amazing, isn't it?"

The town of Paradise Peaks itself was beyond my imagination. It was like something out of a fairy tale. All the buildings were built out of wooden logs, and the entire town resembled a Swiss mountain town. As the car rolled down the street, I soaked in the sights and sounds. The shops were decorated for the holidays already. Christmas decorations filled the windows, the lamp posts were wrapped with lights and garlands, and wreaths were strung over the main street like banners. In the park at the center of the town, stood a giant Christmas tree studded with lights and glittering ornaments. It had to be at least fifty feet tall.

We drove past a horse-drawn carriage clomping along a path in the park. There was a couple sitting in the back of the carriage, snuggled close together under a thick wool blanket.

Finally, we pulled up to a building that looked like a stone castle in the Alps. As soon as we pulled to a stop, two porters rushed out to greet our car and unload our bags.

"Are we where I think we are?" I asked Blake. The Hughes Palace Hotel was a favorite gathering place for celebrities, politicians, and foreign royalty. It was something I had only ever seen in gossip news shows.

"Yes. We're staying at the Hughes in the presidential suite" He exited the car and then helped me out before picking Emilia up in his arms.

We checked in and rode the elevator up to what turned out to be the private entrance to our suite.

"Wow," I said again. Once I stepped out of the elevator, I was greeted with a panoramic floor-to-ceiling window view of the snow-covered mountains that spanned the width of the living room. Just this room was bigger than the entire apartment I shared with Katie.

In the center of the room was a modern glass fireplace with a fire already roaring inside. A decorated Christmas tree stood off to the side near the comfy leather couches. On the opposite side, was an open kitchen. It was fully equipped with fancy professional-grade stainless-steel appliances, an espresso machine, and a bar area.

At the other side of the suite, I spotted an office area through an open door, as well as a series of bedrooms.

Blake let Emilia out of his arms and stretched his back. "You're a writer, Lacey. Surely you can come up with some other description."

I stuck my tongue out at him. "Wow is a perfectly adequate reaction. This place is amazing. It's all ours for the holidays?"

He grinned. "All of it, until after the New Year."

Emilia grabbed my hand. "Let's go pick our rooms."

I laughed and let her drag me down the hall.

After we figured out where we were all going to sleep, it was time for dinner.

We went downstairs to the restaurant in the hotel lobby. The multi-story lobby was tastefully decorated for the holidays. Sparkling crystal ornaments hung above us, recreating the snowy winter wonderland outside. Gold and silver tinsel snaked around the giant bubbling fountain in the middle of the lobby.

The restaurant was more subdued. Each table was covered with a white tablecloth with an arrangement of warm and inviting candles at the center. Jazzy Christmas music played softly in the background. Garlands of pine ran along the dark wooden beams overhead and potted red poinsettia plants added a pop of color all around the dining room.

Emilia was practically bouncing on her feet from the excitement of being somewhere new. Sensing the impending disaster of a hyperactive child in a restaurant filled with delicate glassware and burning candles, Blake picked her up and carried her in one arm.

"Good evening, Mr. Wulfthorn, Mrs. Wulfthorn" the hostess greeted. "Your table is ready. Please follow me."

I shot him a surprised look. My lips parted in surprise, but Blake did nothing to correct her. As we followed the hostess through the restaurant, I scanned the diners in the room. In their crisply tailored suits and expensive silks and pearls, I felt distinctly underdressed in my fleece sweater. Blake reached over and took my hand in his, giving it a comforting squeeze. The warmth from his touch flowed through me, giving me a boost of confidence I didn't know I needed.

We arrived at the rear of the restaurant, where our table overlooked the snow-covered garden at the back of the hotel. After we were seated, the waiter filled our water glasses, and we were presented with our menus and a basket of bread. Our waiter took our drinks orders before disappearing discreetly.

"Don't worry about them, Lacey. There's no dress code here.

It's all fragile egos and small minds. I'm still judged to be lacking."

I took a sip of water. "But how? I mean, you're you."

Blake laughed. "New money has a smell. Not that I give a damn. All money smells good, as far as I'm concerned."

He split open a dinner roll and buttered it before passing it to me. Repeating the motion, he gave half a roll to Emilia and kept the other half for himself. Breaking off a chunk, he chewed for a moment. "Not bad. Baked in house this morning. The crust has a good chew, but it could be crispier."

I bit into the roll and mulled. "Definitely not up to Wulfthorn standards. That's why I took this job, you know. The unlimited supply of fresh bread was an offer I couldn't refuse."

Blake laughed. "That's the sweetest thing anybody's ever said to me. I knew you only wanted me for my buns."

The waiter returned to take our orders. We helped Emilia settle on a five-cheese tortellini in a butter herb sauce. Blake ordered roasted duck with black pepper sauce, while I chose the rack of lamb with garlic and rosemary.

Emilia was so happy to be eating in a big girl restaurant, that she was on her best behavior as she ate her pasta.

"How's your book coming along?" Blake asked before taking a sip of his merlot.

"I'm done with the first draft. Hopefully, I can get in a couple of revisions and send the manuscript to an editor after the new year."

"That's great. I would like to read it when you're finished."

I stabbed a forkful of lamb and paused. "Really? It's just a silly vampire story. You don't have to pretend--"

Blake shook his head. "It's not just a silly story. Don't undersell your talent like that. You have to believe in yourself before others will." He leaned across the table. "Besides, you don't know how many hours of Anne Rice audiobooks I've listened to during my middle-of-the-night baking sessions."

He was right, of course. "Alright then. I'll make sure to save a copy for you and even autograph it."

"Make sure you remember us little people after you have your breakout hit," he added.

I rolled my eyes at him. There was nothing about him that was little.

Outside the window, snow began to fall from the sky in big heavy flakes.

An elderly gentleman with white hair, and kind eyes behind wire-rimmed glasses stopped by our table. He had a large digital camera hanging from a thick strap around his neck. "Oh, this is adorable! I'm so glad to see a young family spending time together."

I smiled awkwardly, unsure of what to say. He was so sincere that I didn't have the heart to correct him. Looking over, I shared a look with Blake. He rose up and reached over the table to shake the old man's hand.

"I'm Blake, and this is Emilia and Lacey."

"I'm George. It's a pleasure to meet you." He held up his camera. "I'm a photographer and I couldn't help noticing how perfectly the atmosphere and the snow outside framed your lovely family. I can take a picture if you'd like?"

"Can we, Lacey?" Emilia asked.

"Yeah, can we, Lacey?" Blake mimicked.

Any reservations I had about this not being real melted at the twin sets of adorable puppy dog eyes staring at me. There was an odd sense of vulnerability and longing in each of their gazes.

"Okay." I turned to George. "How should we pose for the photo, George?"

"Let's see. I think you should stay in your seat while you hold your daughter in your lap. Your husband can stand behind you and lean towards you."

We assumed the pose he described.

George made a swiping motion with his hand. "Blake, can you move closer to your wife and lean over so your arms are around your girls?"

"Like this?" Blake's words came out as a puff of air that tickled my hair. As his arms settled over me like a warm scarf, I was acutely aware of how big and strong he was. A frisson of heat shot up my spine. He completely surrounded me, but instead of feeling smothered, I felt protected and cherished.

"Perfect, now one, two, three, smile and say cheese!" The camera clicked in quick succession. Blake reached down to take my hand in his as he rested his chin near my temple. I looked up at him and the moment our eyes locked, it was as if we were the only ones in the room. Our noses were so close and our breathing synced as one.

"Wonderful!" George exclaimed.

"Can I see?" Emilia kicked her legs and squirmed out of my arms.

I shook my head, falling from the heavens back to reality. My cheeks flushed. What was I thinking? He was my boss, that was all he was going to be. Eager to escape, I followed Emilia and went to see the photos on George's camera.

He scrolled through the pictures and my heart jumped at the small picture of Blake looking at me like I was the most important person in the world.

"I'll send the pictures to you in an email," George said.

Blake and I exchanged our information with George and said our goodbyes after we received the files.

After we finished dinner, we headed back up to our hotel suite. The excitement of the day had finally caught up with Emilia. She was adrift in dreamland not long after I got her into her pajamas and her head hit her pillow.

The last room down the hall was the children's room. I took the middle room while Blake took the room on the other side.

As I crawled under the covers, I pulled out my phone and changed the background wallpaper. On the screen, a miniature version of Blake gazed longingly at me like I was his beloved wife and Emilia was my daughter. I fell asleep staring at a version of my life that could never be real.

CHAPTER 6

BLAKE

While Lacey got Emilia dressed and ready for the day, I finished my phone call. A member of my security team was tailing Fisher and from his intel, the old man spent every day at his horse ranch. It was a good sign, that he wasn't meeting with Unibrod or any other company. I wanted to know the moment he stepped foot in Paradise Peaks. This wasn't quite the same as running through the forest after a rabbit, but I was still a wolf on the hunt. Whether it was a piece of bloody meat or Fisher's signature on a contract, this prey would be mine.

By the time I walked out of my room, Lacey and Emilia were already in the living room. They were sitting on the floor at the coffee table. Emilia was busy doodling on a hotel notepad while Lacey was writing furiously on the backs of Emilia's discarded doodles.

"Is everything okay?" she asked.

I squirmed under Lacey's long gaze. She must have picked up

on my restless energy. In the short time that she had worked for me, we had spent enough time together to learn each other's mannerisms and tell-tale signs of tension.

Forcing myself to put work out of my mind, I shot her an easy grin. "Everything's fine. Just excited to spend the day with my girls."

"Can we go ride the horseys?" Emilia asked.

I sat down next to Lacey and examined Emilia's drawing. It was a mess of scribbles and odd potato-shaped figures with stick limbs, but even I could tell that it was a picture of a small child in between two adult figures. It didn't take a genius to figure out who the three people in the drawing were supposed to be.

"Of course. We can go on a horse carriage ride and even see the big Christmas tree and Santa."

Emilia dropped her pen at the mention of Santa, all thoughts of drawing forgotten. "Santa's here?"

Lacey laughed. "Uh-huh. And all his elves too. You can tell him what you want for Christmas."

"Let's go! Let's go!" Dragging Mr. Snuffles by his ears, Emilia ran to the coat rack and sat down on the wooden bench underneath. She pulled out her snow boots and tried stuffing her feet into the tops.

Lacey giggled at her excitement even as she went to help her with her boots. "Woah, hold on. We have to have breakfast first."

"And then we can go see Santa?" Emilia asked hopefully.

"Yes. Breakfast downstairs first, then we can go visit Santa. I promise," I said.

After breakfast at the hotel restaurant, we walked to the park. Emilia was all too excited to be out after being in the hotel for so long. She skipped and hopped while holding onto Lacey with her left hand and me with her right hand. The shops along the street from the hotel to the park were all festively decorated, and it was nice to disappear into the crowd of people out doing their Christmas shopping.

The town park was full of happy families waiting in line for their children's turn to sit on Santa's lap. A stall nearby was selling roasted cinnamon almonds, filling the air with a wonderful sweet roasted aroma.

Finally, it was Emilia's turn. One of Santa's elves came over to guide Emilia over to Santa. While we waited for Emilia to tell Santa what she wanted for Christmas, a frigid gust of wind blew through. I noticed that Lacey wasn't wearing her scarf today and placed mine around the back of her neck.

She tugged the scarf tightly around her neck and buried her nose in the cashmere as if she was breathing in my scent. Then she closed her eyes and let out a quiet hum of pleasure that only my wolf's sense of hearing could pick up through the noise of the crowd.

A shiver ran down my spine, but it wasn't because of the breeze. There was no way she was drawn to me as I was drawn to her. My cock grew rigid, pulsing with blood as I imagined all the ways I could cover her with my scent. Fill her with my seed. I clenched the edges of my long wool coat around me. There I go again, lusting after my employee like I was a perverted boss. How cliché. What the hell was wrong with me?

Two of Santa's elves helped Emilia off of Santa's knees and

held her hand as they guided her over. Emilia grinned at me and then ran toward Lacey.

Enough. I was too old and my wolf's lust was too depraved for a good woman like Lacey. She was too important to me and to Emilia for me to fuck this up because I couldn't resist the temptation of her flesh and sweet scent. I clenched my jaw. All I had to do was make it after the New Year. Once we were back in Huntington Harbor, we wouldn't have to spend so much time together. I would go back to my office and Lacey would be busy with Emilia.

Lacey picked Emilia up as she ran into her arms. "Did you tell Santa what you want for Christmas?"

Emilia nodded. She glanced at me out of the corners of her eyes before shooting a sly look at Lacey. "It's going to be the best Christmas ever."

I paid the elf for the photo and discreetly pocketed the note he handed me with what Emilia told Santa. Next, we went on a horse-drawn carriage ride around the park. Emilia sat sandwiched between Lacey and me. It was both for her safety and so that my lust-addled mind could cool off.

When we arrived back at the hotel, the lobby was packed with people.

"What's going on?" Lacey asked.

I pointed at the sign next to the doorway to the hotel's ballroom. "It looks like an art exhibit." There were men, women, and children coming in and out of the ballroom. "I think it's open entry. Do you want to check it out?"

Lacey glanced longingly at the exhibit. "I don't know. Emilia might be tired."

Two children, a young boy, about Emilia's age, and an older girl, ran out of the exhibit and raced around the water fountain in the lobby.

Emilia followed them eagerly with her eyes as they dashed across the hotel lobby and back into the exhibit room. "Nuh-uh. I'm not tired. I'm a big girl."

Lacey shrugged. "What do you think?"

It was the first time since the death of her mother that Emilia showed signs of any interest in playing with other children.

I shrugged. "Let's take a quick look before we head upstairs."

Dozens of vibrantly colored abstract paintings hung on the walls of the hotel ballroom. In the center of the room, stood various pieces of sculpture, some of them made of metal and stone, while others looked like a giant rainbow-colored sea anemone made of glass.

Lacey held onto Emilia's hand as she headed toward a painting made up of swirling slashes of blue in various shades.

"It reminds me of the crashing waves of the ocean." She tilted her head as she examined the painting.

I studied the way the brush strokes clashed against each other while moving together in harmony. "It's a reminder of our smallness, that we're all just floating along together, carried by the waves of life."

Lacey hummed in agreement and made a motion tracing the lines of the painting.. "We're all small and adrift, but not alone."

Emilia tugged on the edge of my coat sleeve, interrupting our analysis of the artwork.

"What is it, Emilia?"

She pointed at the corner of the room where it looked like a children's area was set up with miniature easels and drawing paper. The two children who were running around the lobby were there.

"That looks like fun," Lacey said. "Why don't we go see what that's about?"

There was a young woman with the two children. The three of them shared similar eyes and noses. Two siblings and their mother, I deduced.

The older little girl came over first. She carried herself with a confidence that was beyond her age. "Hi, I'm Sorah and that's my brother Will and my mommy."

Emilia clutched at the fabric of my pants and hid behind my legs. Her earlier excitement about meeting new friends faded.

Lacey smiled at the little girl. "It's nice to meet you, Sorah. I'm Lacey, that's Blake, and this is Emilia."

"We're drawing Santa's village. Would you like to help us?"

"Oh, I'm not very good at drawing, but Emilia is." Lacey squatted down to Emilia's height. "Sorah's drawing sounds like a lot of fun. Can we go help her?"

I felt Emilia nod against my leg. Lacey took Emilia's hand in hers and followed Sorah to the easel where her little brother was scribbling vigorously with a marker.

As I watched her play with the two children, a pang of guilt hit me as I realized that this was the first time Emilia had been around other kids. It couldn't be healthy for a child to spend so much time with only adults. I had been so busy with work and barely functioning as her guardian that I had completely neglected her social development.

I heard them coming behind me before I saw them.

"Wulfthorn. I had no idea you were a family man now."

It was Huxley Cain and Derek Fox, alphas of the Huntington Harbor wolf pack. They paused beside me, and together we watched the children with the women who were deep in conversation with each other. It didn't take long for me to put two and two together. These were their pups and their shared mate.

"Cain. Fox." I nodded at them in greeting.

While I had no hard feelings with their pack, we were not exactly on friendly terms. Over the years, they had approached me with an offer to join the pack, but I preferred being a loner. My own family and Reeve were all the wolves I needed in my life.

"Emilia is my niece."

"My condolences to your family. Opal was a formidable she-wolf," Derek said.

I clenched my teeth at the mention of my late sister. Judging by the soft look in his eyes, I could tell that he was being sincere. The two of them had a brief fling in college before they determined that two dominant wolves in a relationship was never going to work out.

"She was taken from us far too soon," I muttered.

Huxley nodded. "That we can agree with." He paused for a moment. "Have you had any luck with the Bean Brewing deal?"

My head shot up.

Derek chuckled. "Everybody in town knows you're gunning for Fisher. You've always been like a rampaging bull in a china shop when it comes to closing a deal."

I let out a growl, hating that they knew me too well despite my efforts to stay under the radar. "He's been avoiding me."

"Fisher's going to be here on Friday. We're having lunch at The Fitzpatrick. Join us." Huxley held up a hand. "Relax. There are no strings attached. You're a lone wolf, and our pack is full as it is. Our kind needs to stick together."

The Fitzpatrick was a private hunting club hidden in the woods in the mountains surrounding Paradise Peaks. It was where politicians, royalty, and the world's leading businessmen made deals that changed society forever. As much as I didn't want to be indebted to anybody, this was my chance to convince Fisher to sell his company to me.

I nodded. "Invitation accepted."

CHAPTER 7

BLAKE

That night, I tossed and turned in bed while I ran through what I wanted to say to Fisher. One way or another, I was going to get him to sell the company to me. It had been years since the violent origins of my first stores. Back then, I didn't have the power or influence that money afforded. What I did have were my fists and fangs. That was enough to convince my competitors to sell their shops to me until I controlled the local market. If the old man wasn't going to see reason, then I was not above going back to my roots to get my way. Still, that was a last resort. Wulfthorn Baked Goods was a legitimate corporation now, and the last thing I needed was a scandal tarnishing my reputation.

I let out a growl and checked the time on my phone. It was almost midnight, and there was no way I was going to get any sleep right now. Giving up any hope of getting rest tonight, I kicked off the covers and went out to the kitchen. There was nothing like a late-night baking session to work out the tension in my body.

It was deathly quiet, so I had to be careful not to make any noise as I gathered my supplies. Thanks to Anna stocking the place before our arrival, I had my favorite flour and baking stone. Most importantly, my treasured sourdough starter was sitting in the fridge ready for me.

As always, the way flour and water mixed together reminded me of how my life started. The ingredients slowly mixed together as I kneaded, the dough turning from a shaggy clumpy pile to a sticky mess before it finally took form and turned into a smooth elastic dough. I scraped the dough into a bowl and put it into the oven with a pan of warm water to rise.

Since there was time to kill before the dough was ready to be shaped, I cleaned up the kitchen. Even over the sound of the water from the kitchen faucet, my wolf's hearing picked up the echo of her footsteps on the tile floor.

I turned off the tap. "I'm sorry for waking you," I said.

I wiped my hands on the kitchen towel next to the sink. Turning around, I gulped. There was no way a woman in loose blue pajamas with penguins all over it should have been so sexy. Her hair was a tousled bedhead, and I wondered if she would look like that in my bed after a night of passion. My fingers bit into my palm as I resisted the urge to grab her and run my hands through those messy strands.

Lacey lifted her glasses off of her nose and rubbed at her eyes. She blinked sleepily at me. "It's not your fault. It takes me a while to get used to sleeping in a new bed. I'm a bit of a night owl."

I smiled. "I hereby welcome you as a member of the insomniac's club."

She sniffed the air and then padded over to the oven and glanced in the window. The oven light inside was on, so she could see the dough rising in the bowl. "Are you baking some bread?"

"A simple sourdough boule."

Lacey shook her head. "There's nothing simple about what you do." She paused. "It's magic to me."

Turning to the espresso machine, I cleared my throat and hid the tingle of pleasure I felt under her words. All the awards and accolades I gained as a world-famous baker failed to compare to her simple words.

"Would you like some coffee? The bread needs time to proof before it's ready to be baked. I can show you how to shape the dough."

"I would like that. Midnight coffee and a snack. You sure know your way to a woman's heart."

"Is through her stomach and her caffeine addiction," I added as I made our coffees.

I joined her at the kitchen counter and we fell into a comfortable silence as we enjoyed our coffees.

"Have you decided the route you're going to take when you publish your novel?" I asked.

Lacey shrugged. "Self-publishing would mean I retain all the rights to my work, but it's hard getting publicity as a first-time author. A traditional publisher would mean I get marketing support, but as a new author, the contract terms are not going to be favorable."

I nodded. She had a kind soul and a gentle heart, and despite her naive appearance, Lacey had a sharp mind for business.

She was my ideal woman. If only she wasn't human and my employee.

"Whatever you decide to do, I can have my lawyers look over the legal contracts when you're ready."

Surprise lit up her eyes. "Thank you," she said softly.

I shrugged. "Your first step in business is the most important one you take. It's best to get off on the right foot."

My phone vibrated, buzzing on the counter. "The dough's ready to be shaped. Are you ready for your first baking lesson?"

Lacey set her cup down and nodded. She jumped to her feet. "Yes, sir. Ready and willing."

I bit back the groan in my throat. My cock sprung to life at her words, tenting my gray sweatpants. There was no hiding my reaction from her. Shit. Thinking quickly, I motioned at the cups. "Why don't you clear the prep area while I go find some aprons for us."

I waited until she was busy at the dishwasher to disappear into the linen closet and retrieve an apron for both of us. Tying the black apron over my front, I fought to bring myself under control before I returned to the kitchen.

Lacey tied the navy blue apron that I gave her. It was entirely oversized on her small figure, making her look even more delicate and defenseless than she really was.

Turning to the oven, I retrieved the proofed dough which was already inflated and threatening to overflow out of the bowl. After I set the bowl on the kitchen counter, I placed the baking stone inside the oven and preheated it.

"Okay, now we need to punch down the dough and shape it

into a boule. Then we're going to let the dough rise a second time before we slash and bake it."

The bag of flour was still on the counter from earlier. I grabbed a fistful of flour and dusted the countertop. With a plastic scraper, I scraped the dough out of the bowl and onto the floured surface.

Crooking my finger, I signaled that she should stand by the counter. I stepped behind her, holding her hands in mine as I showed her how to wet her hands and shape the dough.

"I've never done this before," she said.

"It's easy. Let the flow of the dough guide you," I murmured. "Gently. Stretch, fold, and then roll." Together, we tucked and folded the dough under itself, moving as one unit. Before our eyes, the shapeless dough began to take shape and turn into a smooth tight ball.

"That's it." I grabbed the proofing basket and deposited the formed ball of dough. "Now we wait for the dough to rise again before we put it into the oven."

"Wow! You made that seem so easy," she said as she washed her hands at the sink.

"I've had many years of practice."

I was accustomed to working alone in the kitchen, but tonight I had an audience, and I found that I didn't mind it at all. Once the dough had completed its final rise, I flipped it onto a floured pizza peel and added a few decorative slashes. With a quick jerk of the pizza peel, the bread slid smoothly onto the scorching hot baking stone and I closed the oven door.

Turning around to put the pizza peel down on the counter, I

found Lacey staring at me with a dark hungry look on her face. She clenched the side of the countertop with a white-knuckled grip. Her body was tight with tension as if she was going to pounce at any moment. For the first time in my life, I felt like I was being hunted.

I gulped. A wail from the direction of the bedrooms cut through the silence.

Like a bucket of cold water had been doused over her, Lacey snapped to attention. Once again, she was Emilia's nanny. Her demeanor was completely professional.

"I'll go. She needs me." Lacey rushed out of the kitchen like she was being chased by the hounds of hell.

"Fuck," I muttered under my breath. Running my hands through my hair, I let out a growl.

Disgusted with myself, I went to the kitchen sink to splash cold water on my face. What was I doing? The nanny was off-limits. I should've known better than to play with fire like this. But something about this woman defied all logic and sense. I wanted her, more than anything else I've ever wanted in this life.

Once the bread had finished baking, I pulled it out of the oven and let it rest on a cooling rack.

"She's asleep. It was just a nightmare." Lacey came over and tapped the crust of the bread with her knuckle, making a hollow sound. "Wow. That's beautiful. I can't believe this came from that blob of dough."

"I couldn't have done it without your help." My eyes locked on the smudge of flour on her cheek. "You've got a bit of flour on your face."

"Oh? Where?" She wiped at her cheeks.

"Here, let me." My thumb brushed away the smudge, but I couldn't help running the pad of my thumb over her cheek again.

Her eyes flicked to mine as her breath quickened. Fascinated, I cupped her cheek in my palm, getting my fill of her. She was so warm and soft, sweet and seductive.

She was so soft and smooth, I needed to have my fill of her.

The warmth beneath my palm turned to a searing heat. The beast inside of me roared. Claim her. Take her. Mate her.

I dragged her closer until she could feel my desire for her digging into her stomach. Her luscious lips parted in surprise, and her hands fell to my chest, curling the fabric of my shirt in her grip.

Pulling her closer, my mouth feasted on hers, savoring her flavor. Her lips opened in invitation, as she let out soft moans. Eagerly, my hands traced her body, finally becoming familiar with the curves I had studied for weeks and etched into my memory. Her lush breasts filled my palms perfectly with their heavy weight as if she was made for me. Under my touch, I could feel her heartbeat pulsing like the flapping of a bird's wings. I wanted to wrap my hands around her and possess and control her as much as I wanted to protect her.

Her tongue met mine hungrily, stroke for stroke, and I thrust my tongue into her mouth, showing her what I wanted to do to her with my cock. She let out a low guttural moan, opening herself for more. The scent of her arousal blossomed around us, covering both of us in her sweet musk.

Lacey was so responsive. Her passionate desire was beyond

my wildest dreams. I had a hunch that the slightest touch could push her over the edge. And that's what I did.

Sliding my hand down the front of her pajamas, I searched for the source of her desire. She was burning hot and slippery as I slipped my fingers between her thighs. Her little nubbin was swollen and hard as a cherry.

I wondered how many strokes of my fingers it would take until she gushed her juice all over me. What an interesting experiment. As I worried the sensitive bit of flesh, she sucked in a breath and bit down on my lip. The bitter metallic tang of my blood hit my tongue, flaming my wolf's bloodlust. Sex and pain were one and the same for my kind. Faster and faster, I rubbed her, coaxing more dew from her core.

Finally, she wrenched her lips away from mine. Looking up at me and holding my gaze, she rocked her hips against the heel of my hand.

"Good girl." I grinned wickedly at her as she started fucking herself on my hand. Her mouth hung open as she panted and climbed towards her climax. Sensing that she was close, I pulled my other hand back and gave a series of quick sharp slaps to her bottom. She yelped and cried out her release as she went stiff and exploded, gushing all over my hand.

The sight of her coming undone was almost enough to make me spurt my seed all over myself like a teenager.

She looks up at me in a daze as she comes down from her orgasm. I brought my hand up to my mouth and licked each of my fingers clean of her honey. The taste of her on my tongue ignited a primal urge inside of me. My vision turned red. The beast roared, clawing at my insides to take what was mine.

I gripped her bottom in my hand, squeezing hard enough to leave a mark. Her yelp was like a bucket of ice water dumped over my head. I pushed myself away from her.

What kind of monster was I? Lacey was far too delicate and important to treat like a bitch in heat that I was about to fuck on the kitchen counter.

"What about you?" She reached out for me, but I intercepted her. Bringing her hand up, I kissed her knuckles.

Repressing the beast's demands to mount her, I dug my nails into my palms. "It's late. Emilia wakes up early. Go get some rest," I ground out.

Like a coward, I ran away with my tail between my legs to the refuge of my room. Pressing my body against the back of the door, I waited until I heard the snick of her own bedroom door closing and locking.

"Idiot," I muttered under my breath. For the first time ever, my life was in complete harmony. Family and work fit together and it was all with Lacey's help. What I just did tonight put all of that in jeopardy. Not only did Emilia think of her as family, but she was human for fuck's sake. That should have been enough to put a stop to all of this. A female human could not withstand the violence and perversion a wolf demanded when he rutted his mate.

Because that was what she was, I realized with a jolt. It explained the powerful pull she had over me and the way my wolf was lulled to sleep when she was around. That was, when the wolf wasn't aroused into a roaring rage to claim her. What a cruel twist of fate that she wasn't a she-wolf.

The claiming was what scared me. The wolf itched to take every bit of her pussy, ass, and mouth. We would rut over and over again until my seed spilled from her. I would fill her until she was ruined for any other man, then mark her with my handprints and my bite so that every wolf knew she was mine.

It was brutal and animalistic. It would break her frail human body. It could never be.

I let out a growl and punched the pillows on my bed. Even through the walls between us, I could sense her. Against my own will, my hand came up to my nose and I gave it a good long whiff. Having her scent all over me wasn't making it easy to resist the temptation of the mate that I could never have.

With my cum churning in my nuts, and a denied release, I was never going to get any sleep. Stripping out of my clothes, I reached down and gripped my cock. If I couldn't have my sweet innocent nanny in real life, then I would have to settle for imagining Lacey taking all of my cock until my balls plugged her as I filled her with my seed.

"Fuck, that's it. Take me," I groaned as I pumped my hand up and down my shaft. She was now on her knees, offering her pretty little mouth for me. I tugged at my cock, imagining it was her throat I was plunging into. Faster and faster I tugged. Then she was on her hands and knees, her head to the floor and her bubble butt bouncing as she took me in her ass and I marked her bottom with my handprints.

My cum dripped from my cock, mimicking her slick dew across my shaft. Once, twice, and then my cock jerked as I came, filling her dark channel before I sprayed her ass and back with my seed.

As I opened my eyes, the last spurts of my cum landed on my barren bedsheet. The orgasm took the edge off, but I was still throbbing with need. Grabbing the edge of the sheet, I pulled it off and dumped it in a pile on the floor. My fantasies were a pale substitute for the real thing, but it would have to do. I collapsed on the bed and fell into an uneasy sleep with my mind haunted by thoughts of a sweet little nanny who could never be mine.

CHAPTER 8

LACEY

Emilia waved at me from across the room as she watched the model train snake around the store with a group of other children. Despite her heavy winter jacket making her look like a puffy marshmallow, she insisted on bringing Mr. Snuffles with her, which she clutched in the crook of her arm.

I smiled and waved back. The entire store was a wonderland of everything Christmas. Around displays of candy canes, giant wooden nutcrackers, and tinsel-covered trees, the train chugged along before circling back to the center of the store where there was a model train set that was a miniature recreation of Paradise Peaks.

Keeping my eye on Emilia, my mind drifted to what happened last night in the kitchen. After so many days of longing and repressing my desires, Blake finally confirmed that he was falling in love with me as much as I was falling in love with him. My entire body tingled with heat at the memory of his touch. I clenched my thighs as a rush of warmth rushed from my belly to my core. He had strummed my body like we had been lovers all our lives, and he knew just what got me off. Even now, I could still taste the faint flavor of him on my lips.

I had been so sure that we were going to make love last night, but something spooked him at the last minute. My mind raced through what it could have been. By the time I woke up this morning, he was already gone from the apartment, leaving only a brief handwritten note as an explanation. The loaf of bread we made together was the only evidence that any of it had happened.

Nothing was going to be the same from now on. Everything had changed. He could run and hide, but I knew him now. Knew how he tasted. Knew how he felt pressed against my body. We had to talk.

Emilia was still engrossed with the train just like the rest of the children, so I took the time to examine a display of ornaments next to me. Shopping for Christmas presents was the exact distraction I needed at the moment.

Among the collection of standard reindeer, angel, and globe ornaments, there were some unique ones in the mix. I had no idea what to get a billionaire who already had everything, but the little bread loaf ornament was exactly what I was looking for.

Snatching one of the ornaments off of the hook on the display, I quickly went to the cashier's counter nearby. After I paid, I waited for the employees behind the counter to wrap the ornament. For Emilia, I already commissioned a crochet bunny hat from Katie before the trip. Her present was already waiting to be placed under the tree in our hotel apartment. I took the wrapped ornament and happy that all of my Christmas shopping was now done, I went over to join the Emilia.

That evening, we had a quiet dinner at home. Blake ordered a complete seafood feast from the restaurant downstairs. The chef from the restaurant came up to our suite to personally set the table for us. Our dinner was served family style and contained multiple main dishes, including a seafood medley pasta, lobster tails, and grilled halibut. We also had a delicious lobster bisque which we ate with the bread we baked last night. Despite my fears that a child would be squeamish about so many exotic foods, Emilia was distracted by telling Blake about her exciting day at the store with the choo-choo train.

As we ate, I couldn't help but glance at Blake. He was too engrossed by his niece's tales to acknowledge me, or at least he pretended to be. The tension of what was left unsaid was palpable in the air. By the time Emilia was in bed, I was ready to explode with the need to confront Blake about what happened last night.

Blake had finished cleaning up and started the dishwasher when I walked back into the kitchen. I knew he heard me come in, but he kept pretending that he needed to wipe down the gleaming countertop. He was avoiding me, I knew it. While I was afraid of poking the beast, I had to know the truth.

"Do you find me repulsive?" Last night was one of the best moments of my life, but if it meant that I had ruined the blossoming friendship between us and the bond I had with Emilia, then I wished it hadn't happened at all. "We can pretend none of it happened and let everything go back to normal. I don't want this to impact my relationship with

Emilia. The last thing that child needs in her life is instability."

Blake's head snapped up, his eyes searching mine. "You're many things, Lacey, but the last thing I would've pegged you for is a fool."

I opened my mouth, but before I could protest, he sighed deeply and continued. "You're right that we should pretend nothing happened and go back to normal after this trip."

My heart shattered as he spoke. Swallowing the lump in my throat, I blinked away the moisture in my eyes. I was damned if I was going to let him see how much his words hurt.

"Because you have utterly ruined me, Lacey Conway. When I am with you, it's like nothing else in the world exists. The power you have over me scares me to the core." He closed the distance between us in two strides. Cupping my cheeks in his hands, he held my gaze. "You make me lose control, and I fucking hate it. But I love you."

I didn't know it was possible to fly from the depths of despair to the heights of euphoria in a single moment. My head felt like I was drunk as I processed what he was telling me.

"I love you too, Blake," I whispered.

Electricity sizzled between us. Looming over me, his copper eyes flashed darkly. I could feel the heat rising from his body.

"I need you to be sure because I will have all of you. Once I make you mine, there is no turning back."

"Please, make me yours."

In one swift motion, he swung me up in his arms and carried me to his room where he tossed me onto the bed. With movements faster than I could follow, he made quick work of tugging off my clothes. I tried to help him undress, but he batted my clumsy hands away with impatience.

Towering over me, I was acutely aware of our size difference. He was a giant who could break me with a single hand. I was completely at his mercy. Soon he was upon me, wrapping my hair in his hand as he held me in place. Hungrily, I returned his kiss. While he kept me pinned as he devoured my mouth, his other hand explored my body with a possessive touch. Cupping and kneading my breast, he teased my nipples with his thumb until they stood tight and hard for his touch.

Suddenly, he broke our kiss, leaving me bereft and cold. Before I could react, he dropped to his knees and gripping my thighs, he tugged me until my butt was on the edge of the bed and my legs slung over his shoulders.

My hips jolted up at the first touch of his tongue on my clit. Blake let out a warning growl that buzzed through my womb. His fingers tightened around my thighs until I was sure he was going to leave five bruises on each side. Without mercy, he worried my clit with his tongue with firm and insistent swipes.

I cried out, unable to do anything but succumb to the pleasure he wrung out of my body. My hands gripped his hair, pulling him closer to my core. Deeper. More. I wanted all of him inside of me. As if he heard my unspoken wish, he plunged three fingers into my channel, stretching me to my limits as he twisted his fingers and pumped them into me. If his fingers felt this big, then what was it going to feel like when he fucked me with his cock?

Blake soothed away the pain, doubling his efforts on my clit.

I arched my back, screaming and pleading for him to let me

come. My hips bucked against his face, eager for more pressure on my sex.

Cruelly, he kept me teetering on the edge of completion until I was on the verge of tears. While he fucked me with one hand, he drew his other hand through the slickness dripping down my folds and nudged his thumb against my ass.

Light exploded behind my eyelids as I came. My body thrashed on the bed while I rode the waves of pleasure.

As I came back down to earth, Blake tore off his clothes. I gasped when his rock-hard cock sprung free from his pants. It was massive, thickly veined, and an angry shade of red. My sex throbbed at the sight.

Gripping both of my ankles in one hand, he tugged them until my legs were bent over my head. With my butt exposed, he gave me a series of sharp slaps, some of them landing on my bottom, while others landed with a wet squelch on my sex.

The sensations were too much and the blows stung, but it only made my core clench with pleasure. I squirmed, but he was too strong. I couldn't get away. Then, with one quick motion, he lifted my hips and plunged his swollen shaft into my slick channel.

There was a burning sensation as his thick head slipped past my outer lips, but I was so slick that he slid in without resistance. For a moment, he held me still, forcing me to stretch around his invading cock. I pulsed around him, gripping him like I was made for him. Then he pulled back and slammed in, his heavy balls slapping against my plump lips. I cried out at the jolt of pleasure and clenched my eyes shut. He stretched me to the point of splitting, piercing me to the mouth of my womb with each drive of his cock into me.

It felt so good, as he stretched the walls of my sex, spearing me until he bottomed out. There was nothing I could do but take it as he impaled me over and over again with his dick. I grew lightheaded with the pleasure soaking every last inch of my body. I clenched my muscles, squeezing his member in time with each stroke.

Faster and faster he pumped. It was impossible, but I swore I could feel him grow bigger inside of me, pulsing and swelling. I forced my heavy eyes to open and met his gaze.

He grunted as he rocked into me. "I can't pull out now. You're going to take it all, every last drop." His eyes seemed to glow with unnatural fire as he fucked me. These were the eyes of a beast consumed with the need to mate.

"Yes, give it to me," I panted. I bore down, milking him, adding to the dark decadent pain of our mating.

Blake roared before slamming into me brutally. I came instantly, convulsing as he filled my passage with his seed until it gushed out and dripped over both of us. Together we rode out our pleasure, losing control as we gave into our animalistic urges. It went on for an eternity. Eventually, I could take no more and he collapsed bonelessly on top of me.

We lay there, warm and drowsy with satisfaction. I realized he was still inside of me. Completely hard and swollen.

I gaped at him in shock. "How are you still hard?"

He laughed as he pulled out of me and released my legs. I winced at the tightness in my muscles. His dick was coated in our combined desire and it jutted out and bobbed as he kneeled between my thighs. "I told you I was going to have all of you."

Reaching down, he ran his hand along my puffy lips, swirling his fingers through the spendings pooled there before bringing them up to swirl them on my clit.

I moaned as he stroked me, igniting the fire in my core once again. When he teased the opening of my sex, I hissed. "My poor girl, you're all red and swollen. I was too rough with you."

Despite the painful sting, I rocked my hips and begged for more. Lust overwhelmed all of my senses as pleasure spread through every inch of my body once again. "I need you again."

Blake shook his head. "You do not know your limits, my love." He withdrew his hand and stood up. I let out a pitiful cry in protest.

"Relax. I have a solution." Handling me like I was a rag doll, he manipulated me until I lay on the bed with my head hanging over the edge. He leans over me and pries my knees apart. "Keep these spread for me."

At that moment, I realized that I was at the perfect height to suck his cock. My mouth watered. Straining my neck, I reached for him, taking his fat rod in my mouth. I moaned at the saltiness of him, savoring the weight of his cock against my tongue.

"Good girl, suck me hard," he grunted.

I followed his order to the best of my ability, licking and stroking with my tongue. His hips rocked, pressing gently but insistently, as he fed more and more of his cock into my mouth. Soon, I took him all the way to the hilt, swallowing around him as he slipped down my throat.

As he fucked my mouth, he kept up his relentless teasing of my clit. Mindful of the soreness in my sex, he massaged me tenderly as he spread my slickness down my folds until he circled and rimmed my bottom. And then, I felt him there, pressing an insistent finger against my tight back hole.

I moaned in protest, but I was pinned by his cock. There was nothing I could do against this pleasurable onslaught. He spread more of my dew on my sphincter and then pressed again. This time, he kept pushing until his entire finger slipped in past the first knuckle. I wiggled my bottom, but that only wedged his digit deeper in and earned me a sharp slap on my thigh.

"Every part of you belongs to me now." Blake withdrew his finger and pulled his hips back. He paused for a moment before pushing both back in, this time stretching my tight ring of muscles with two fingers. "Behave and I will make this feel good for you."

I squirmed while he began fucking me at both ends. This was the first time I had ever had anything up my ass, and to my dark delight, it began to feel good. The more he teased and stretched my ass, the better it felt. The soreness and pain melted away, leaving only warm pleasure.

Blake withdrew his fingers and pulled his cock out of my mouth with a pop.

I moaned in protest. Just when he was getting close to flooding my mouth with his salty seed, he denied me my reward.

"You're ready." He lifted me then flipped me over and positioned me on my hands and knees facing away from him.

Instinctively, I arched my back like a cat, presenting myself to my lover. He fumbled for something on the nightstand. I nearly purred as he pinned me in place from behind with a hand on the back of my neck.

I felt the cold squirt of something on my lower back. A sweet almond scent enveloped us and I realized it was some kind of oil. He massaged my tight muscles, working the oil down into my cleft. The tip of his cock traced a path from my clit up to my ass, then he slipped along my folds, so close to fucking me, but not quite. At that moment, I had complete trust that he wouldn't hurt me. I was his. I had to submit to the pleasure he bestowed upon me.

He applied the oil to his shaft, and then waited patiently, pressing the thick swollen head against my virgin hole.

The hand at my nape stroked me gently, brushing my hair to the side. "You can do it. Be a good girl, and let me into that tight little ass."

"I don't know if I can," I panted. My heart raced. Even the tip of him was too big. He stretched my sex to the limit, how was he going to fit into my ass?

"You don't have to know, just trust me."

While he kept me pinned in place, his other hand stroked my flanks, as if reassuring me. Rocking his hips slightly, he prodded my sphincter, each time pressing harder and longer against the tight muscle. I closed my eyes and took a deep breath. He was right. I had to trust him. I bore down, and on the next push, he slipped past the resistance. The ridge of his shaft popped in and slowly, he fed his entire length into my bottom.

Blake hissed. "Yes. You take my cock so well. Every part of you, from your mouth and your pussy filled with my seed, to your tight little bottom, was made for this."

I strained under the tight pressure. He felt even bigger than when he fucked me the normal way. I could feel every ridge of the veins on his shaft as he impaled my untried ass. My fingers clenched the bedsheets until I was sure they were going to tear.

Blake paused. "Almost there. I'm halfway in. Just a bit more, my love." His breath was labored as he spoke.

I gasped. No way. He was already piercing me to the heart, or at least that's what it felt like. Taking all of him was going to split me apart!

My hips squirmed, but there was no escape. I was locked in the prison of his muscles and overwhelming strength.

He reached down to stroke my swollen clit, and then with one final forceful push, he plunged all the way in, his balls slapping against my wet puffy lips.

The warmth rushing from my sensitive nub battled with the soreness in my ass. He stroked me in time with each thrust, mixing the pain and pleasure until I was unable to separate which was which.

Faster and harder he took me, pushing me up higher and higher toward the peak.

"Your little ass looks so beautiful stretched around my cock," he murmured.

It hit me suddenly, my orgasm rocking through my body, shattering me into a million pieces. Every part of me seized as I rode out the shockwaves.

Blake let out a roar. "Mine!" he growled.

He pulled me upright, bringing my neck to his mouth. I cried out at the sharp bite of his teeth in my neck. Impaled on his teeth and cock, I spasmed helplessly as I came again. He pumped one final time into me, his cock swelling and twitching. Then I felt the jets of his seed spurting into me. My muscles tightened, milking every last drop out until he filled me to bursting and I could feel his cum dripping out.

He slipped out, finally spent. Gently, he placed me on the bed and disappeared into the bathroom before returning with a warm washcloth. After he cleaned me, he climbed into bed next to me and placed a kiss on my forehead.

"You are perfect in every way, Lacey."

I blushed under his praise and nuzzled into his chest.

He tipped my head up and claimed my lips. When we broke apart, I smiled lazily in contentment. "I am so happy, Blake. Promise we will always be like this."

"I promise."

CHAPTER 9

BLAKE

I woke up to what seemed to be a dream. Lacey was in my arms, snoring cutely against my chest. She was my mate. Was this even real? The beast inside me roared in triumph. She was mine. At the same time, my heart soared with happiness.

There was only one thing that dampened my mood this morning. It was Friday, which meant I had to leave her and Emilia to go meet with Fisher. After pursuing him for months, I was so close to my goal. Yet, I didn't give a shit about the coffee company one bit if it meant I had to be away from my family.

Over breakfast, Lacey seemed to sense my unease. "This is the moment you've been waiting for. You'll never forgive yourself if you don't go for it and do your best."

She nudged Emilia with her elbow. "Besides, we girls are going to Santa's village and see the reindeer, today. We'll still be here waiting for you when you come back from work."

Emilia nodded. "I'm going to meet all the elves and ride on the reindeer," she announced around a mouthful of pancakes.

I chuckled. "Well, maybe you can feed the reindeer. I don't think they'll like you riding on them."

Lacey was right. I had to do this. This company had to grow to the next level in order to last into the next generation. It was for my family's sake. I had to remember why I was doing this.

When I walked into the private club to Huxley and Cain's table, Fisher almost leaped out of his seat. His face was twisted in surprise, and fear. Not only did he not know I was coming, but he was also afraid of me for some reason.

After some small talk and shooting the shit over our drinks, Cain and Huxley made an excuse to leave the table. I was finally all alone with Fisher.

There was no use pretending or beating around the bush. I cut straight to the chase. "You and both know why I am here. Neither of us is going to leave this table until you agree to sell the company to me."

The old man threw back his head and downed his entire glass of whiskey in a single gulp. "I can't do that, Wulfthorn."

I growled and banged my fist on the table. "Why the fuck not? How much is Unibrod offering you for the company?"

He scoffed. "Not enough."

"Then why won't you hear me out?"

Fisher sighed. His tired eyes looked down at the table and at that moment, every decade of his age was written in the lines of his face. "Unibrod is threatening me with a secret that's supposed to be buried and dead. My daughter is engaged to

Senator Norton's son. I can't let this come out. It would destroy my family."

I frowned. It all made sense now. Fisher was being blackmailed.

"If I get Unibrod off of your back, will you agree to sell to me?"

Fisher paused. "Then we can talk business. I'm sure you know how they work. After all, they are your kind too, Wulfthorn."

I nodded. Unibrod was run by the Nightblood wolf pack. Based out of London, the tentacles of their syndicate ran deep and wide all over the world, aided by their ties to the Russian mob and the vampire clans. If I tried to take them on, I was potentially bringing on the wrath of multiple powers.

"I'll handle it."

After my meeting with Fisher, I decided to head back home. While Pete, my driver, weaved through the mountainous roads leading back to Paradise Peaks, I called Reeve.

"Hey. Fisher's willing to sell if we take down Unibrod. He's being blackmailed."

"Are you going to go ahead?" Reeve asked.

"Yes."

He paused. For a moment, I didn't know if my business partner was going to go along with this. He knew full well the risks of what I was proposing.

Reeve let out a long sigh. "Only a multinational take down.

No big deal. I'll keep an eye out for the Nightbloods and figure something out."

I paused, unsure if I should tell him. Reeve was like a brother to me. Though we were not related, we shared a bond that rivaled that created by blood.

"Dude, what's up?"

"I'm mated," I blurted out.

"How?" Reeve asked. His tone was incredulous. "Is it the nanny?"

My silence revealed the answer.

Reeve laughed. "Ha! I knew it. You've been weird for weeks once she showed up. Congrats, dude."

"Thanks, Reeve. I owe you."

A beeping tone on the phone interrupted our call. I looked at the phone and frowned. It was Mark, my other driver, who was supposed to be bringing Emilia and Lacey home from the reindeer farm by now.

"I have to take this call."

"Sir, there was an accident. Someone ran our car off the road. Miss Emilia and Miss Lacey--"

My heart plummeted. No...

At that moment, my car drove through a tunnel, disconnecting the call.

"Fuck!" I screamed. As soon as we emerged from the tunnel, I called him back.

"Where are you? Are they okay?"

"Yes. They're shaken, but nobody's hurt."

I tapped on Pete's shoulder. He nodded and signaled that he was going to pull into the trailhead parking lot coming up. Immediately, I put the phone on speakerphone.

"Where are you?" I repeated.

"Pinenut Pass, just beyond the ski resort."

My driver swung into the parking lot and spun the car around with a loud screech of tires. We had just driven past the junction to Pinenut Pass.

"Stay there and keep them safe," I commanded. "I'm on my way."

I opened the door and jumped out of my car before it came to a full stop. My girls were sitting on a rock next to the side of the road. Lacey held Emilia in her arms, rocking her as she cried. Their car had crashed into a large pine tree. The front was crushed into the tree trunk and the rear was damaged too.

Rushing over to my family, I ran my hands over Lacey and Emilia, checking them for any injuries. Lacey had a cut on her forehead that was already swelling. I brushed my thumb across her temple. The trail of blood from the cut had dried and crusted already. At last, I was satisfied with my examination and pulled them tightly into my arms.

"I could have lost you," I whispered. My voice shook as I spoke. "Both of you."

"We're okay," Lacey murmured. "Mark handled the car like a pro. We got out unscathed."

"What happened?"

"A black car followed us from the farm. Mark noticed them and tried to shake them off, but then they rammed into us. Thank God this stretch of the road wasn't next to a cliff."

It still wasn't safe, I thought. We were sitting ducks on the side of the road. I had to get them home. Lifting Emilia in one arm, I helped Lacey to her feet with my other. We walked over to my car and I ushered them into the back seat.

While I had tended to my girls, Pete had helped Mark to the front passenger seat of the car. Mark was walking with a limp and he cradled his left arm to his chest with his right one.

"How are you?" I asked.

"I'm fine," he mumbled.

Pete shared a look with me that indicated he disagreed. I nodded. "Go to the hospital. All of them need to be checked out."

Mark grabbed my arm. "Boss, whoever followed us was a pro."

It was almost midnight by the time Lacey, Emilia, and Mark were cleared by the doctors. Mark had suffered two cracked ribs and a broken arm from the impact. He refused an overnight stay at the hospital for monitoring and insisted that he only needed to go to his hotel room to sleep it off. Lacey suffered a minor cut from the glass shattering and scraping her forehead. Thankfully, neither she nor Emilia were seriously injured.

As soon as we stepped into the lobby, the front desk staff handed me an express mail envelope. It was addressed to me at the hotel. Strange, but not important at the moment. The only thing I had to concern myself with was getting Lacey and Emilia home.

Lacey was given ibuprofen for any pain resulting from the crash. I was on orders from the doctors to watch both of them for any signs of concussion.

Once they were in bed and I was alone, I opened the envelope. It was a simple typed letter with two sentences.

Stay away from Fisher. Next time, your family will be at the bottom of a ravine.

I crushed the letter in my fist. It was the fucking Nightblood wolves. It had to be. I had been so distracted with tailing Fisher that I had not considered that Unibrod's lackeys were following us the entire time we were in Paradise Peaks. I had slipped up and it almost cost Lacey and Emilia their lives.

And Fisher wasn't my only distraction, a voice in my head whispered. As much as I loved Lacey, she was still a human. A weak point that would be easily exploited by my enemies. Unlike a she-wolf, Lacey was completely defenseless. This was what I had always feared. At that moment, I knew what I had to do.

I let out an anguished cry and went to the mini bar. Not caring about anything else, I drank straight from the bottle of vodka.

"Blake?" Lacey's soft voice pierced through the fog of anguish in my head.

She came up behind me and touched my shoulder. I shook her off and put distance between us.

I paced the room before I stopped and stared out the window. "We have to talk, Lacey." The words flowed out of my mouth despite my wolf screaming and clawing at my insides. "We've been moving too fast. I think we should take a break."

"What do you mean?"

I didn't need to turn around to know her chin was quivering as she spoke. It was like I was having an out-of-body experience. Unable to control what was happening, I watched the scene play out like it was a movie.

I took another swig of liquor for courage. "It was a mistake." My mind flashed back to Lacey sitting on the side of the road with the wreckage of the accident behind her. "We were never going to work out. You were hired to be the nanny. Your only job is to take care of my niece, not jump into my bed."

"Is that all you have to say?"

I swallowed the lump in my throat as the bitter words flowed out. "I think that concludes our meeting."

"You're such an ass." She stormed back to her room.

I waited until she slammed the door behind her before I threw the bottle across the room. It exploded against the wall and rained a thousand shards of glass onto the floor, just like my heart.

For the rest of the week, Lacey avoided me like the plague, only acknowledging my existence when prompted by Emilia. Her attention was focused solely on my niece. Even through her hurt, she was a professional. It was exactly what I asked her to do, but the coldness in her eyes every time she looked at me cut like glass.

We were like ghosts inhabiting the same apartment. What

was supposed to be a joyous holiday was now laced with bitterness.

Since Unibrod's men were still out there, I didn't allow Lacey or Emilia to leave the hotel suite. Not even the hotel common areas downstairs were safe.

Emilia was starting to act up from being cooped up. She was regressing and today, it took Lacey two hours to convince her to eat her breakfast. I looked over at the shimmering Christmas tree and wondered what happened to our happy little family that was too short-lived.

My phone vibrated and lit up. It was Reeve.

"What is it?"

"Is that how you greet your newest favorite person?" Reeve teased.

I scoffed. "Who says that's you?"

"I will be very soon. Call down to the front desk and buzz me up, dude."

I tapped on the intercom unit on the wall and ordered the front desk to give Reeve the code to our floor.

What was he going on about now and why was he here in Paradise Peaks? But I was eager for a distraction from the silence of the apartment.

The elevator dinged before the doors opened and Reeve stepped out. He walked into my office and closed the door behind him.

Wordlessly, he grabbed the TV remote and flipped through the channels until the stock exchange floor popped up. One of the female talking heads flashed onto the screen.

"We have some breaking news. Unibrod Corporation stock has just been halted." The anchor paused as she listened to her earpiece. "Sources say there has been a raid by the authorities. All Unibrod facilities in the United States are to be shut down pending investigation."

I was stunned. "Did you have something to do with this?"

Reeve flashed a cocky grin. "What? Like it was hard? It didn't even take me two days to hack into Ulf Nightblood's computer." The joy in Reeve's voice was unmistakable. Like myself, he was stifled by the rules and laws we now had to abide by and itched to return to his unlawful origins. "The Nightbloods have skirted laws and regulations in every country they have operated in. It was only a matter of time before someone, *ahem*, ratted them out to the feds."

This was it. The moment we had been waiting for. We finally had leverage over the Nightbloods to make them back off, both from Fisher and from my family. I should have been ecstatic. So why was I numb?

Reeve glanced at me expectantly. The grin on his face slowly vanished. He waved his hand back and forth in front of my face. "Hello? Dude, what's wrong with you?"

"I ended it with Lacey," I mumbled.

He stared at me before punching me on the shoulder. "That's stupid, even for a doughhead like you."

I shrugged him off. "She's human, Reeve. You know what that means. Nightblood put a hit on her."

"Yeah, so what? Do you know how rare a true mate match is? Some of us go our entire lives without finding our mate, and here you are, pissing it all away because she's not a pure-blooded female wolf."

"That's not what I mean," I protested. "You know I hate that type of thinking. I'm nothing like my parents."

Reeve cut me off. "No? You still sound like them at the moment. We live dangerous lives, and now you've left her completely defenseless. If you want to keep her safe, then tell her the truth about our kind. Show her our world and prepare her for the threats. You know there's no backing out of a mating claim. You are the only one who can defend her now." Reeve paused his rant and let out a long breath. "Look, she's your mate. Nothing else matters."

He was right. Of course, Reeve was always right. "I have to talk to her."

"Damn, right you do. Go get your woman."

I exited the office to find the kitchen was empty. Emilia was in her room by herself, coloring with Mr. Snuffles.

"Emilia, where's Lacey?"

She shrugged. "Out."

My stomach dropped. Something was wrong. "Did she say where she was going?"

Emilia shook her head.

Fuck.

Reeve came in and sat down at the kids' play table where Emilia was coloring. "Go find her, Blake. I'll watch the kid."

Faster than I thought possible, I went downstairs and raced through the lobby. I called both of my drivers, but neither of them knew where Lacey was. That meant she was traveling by foot. The only places close enough to the hotel were the shopping area in town, and the lake near the hotel.

Suddenly, a searing pain twisted my gut. I doubled over. It was unlike anything I had ever felt in my life. A sense of foreboding overcame my entire body.

"Lacey," I whispered. It was the mate bond. She was in trouble.

Relying on my wolf's connection with my mate, I ran toward the woods by the lake. The tops of the trees swayed softly in the wind, obscuring what was happening down on the ground.

It was too hard to track her this way. My human form dulled my senses and would only slow me down. Reeve's words echoed in my mind. I had to tell her the truth about what I was.

Triggering the change, I howled as muscles twisted and bones snapped as they changed shape. With sharp claws, I ripped at my clothes, tearing what wasn't already destroyed by the shift.

Soon, all the colors in front of me took on a new dimension. Smells and sounds were magnified a hundred times, to the point of being overwhelming. I dropped onto all fours as the shift completed its course.

Running toward the trees, I sniffed the air for her scent. It was faint, blown away by the wind, but I smelled her. My paws pounded on the dirt, as I let my nose and the mate bond guide me through the forest. With only the speed and agility of a wolf, I dashed between the trees and up the mountain. Finally, I spotted them. Lacey was sprawled on the ground, shivering in the snow with a large gray wolf on top of her.

Lacey's cries of fear made my vision turn red. I pounced on

his back, knocking him away from her. At that moment, there were no more thoughts in my mind. I was pure anger and rage. All I wanted was his blood flowing down my throat as I ripped his neck out.

The wolf rolled from under me, jumping into the air to avoid the swipe of my claws.

I kicked at him with my hind legs, landing a satisfying blow. He flew into a nearby tree, his bones cracking from the impact. The wolf recovered and lunged at me again. This time, I was prepared. Aiming high, my claws tore through his side.

He fell in a heap on the ground. I landed on top of him, biting down on his throat and landing the final blow. Blood flowed from his torn neck like a bright red fountain.

The gray wolf gurgled one last time before the life faded from his eyes.

It was over. The chill of the winter wind blowing on my blood-soaked face replaced the heat of battle. I glanced up from my vanquished enemy to find Lacey looking at me with fear in her eyes.

As the last of the rage subsided, I shifted back into my human form.

At that moment, I realized what I looked like. I was a monster. An inhuman beast. Crouched there on the dirt and snow, I was too afraid to look up at her. I didn't want to see the disgust on her face now that she knew what I really was.

"Blake," she said softly. She kneeled down next to me and traced her fingers down the ridge of my brow, and down along my cheek, getting the wolf's blood all over her hands. Her touch was reverent.

I held my breath until she wrapped her arms around me and pulled me in for a kiss. My mate's acceptance of me, wolf and man, was like a healing balm on my tortured soul.

"I'm so sorry," I whispered, my voice cracking. I ran my hands down her body. "Are you hurt?"

She shook her head. "He didn't have time to do anything."

"I almost lost you."

"Shh," Lacey silenced me with a finger on my lips. "You saved me. We can talk later."

I carried her through the forest and back to the hotel. We went in through the employee entrance. The hotel was used to dealing with high-powered guests and looking the other way. They were not going to gossip about the naked blood-covered billionaire who stumbled in from the snow.

Once we were upstairs, Lacey and Reeve worked as a team to distract Emilia and shield her from my frightful state. After I cleaned myself up, Reeve went home, and I spent a quiet night at home, snuggled together on the sofa with my girls in my arms as we watched The Lion King. Bending my head, I placed a kiss on top of Lacey's head. I was never going to let her go again.

As long as I was alive, I was going to protect them, even if it cost me my life.

CHAPTER 10

LACEY

I was woken up by the excited yelling of a little girl. Blinking sleepily, I groaned and rubbed at my eyes. Next to me, Blake picked up his phone to check the time. "It's not even seven yet, how can she be so bright-eyed and bushy-tailed?" He grunted and rolled over, hiding his face in his pillow.

"I would kill to have as much energy as a four-year-old," he grumbled, his voice muffled by his pillow.

With a laugh, I threw back the covers and revealed his taut peach of a bottom, which I tapped playfully before getting out of bed. "She's never going to forgive you if you make her wait too long to open her presents."

Some time during the night when we had been asleep, it had started snowing. The mountains outside were covered in white caps, and the pine trees glistened with the fresh snowfall. Snow flakes were still falling, giving a magical feeling to our snowy white Christmas.

Blake gave a resigned sigh as I went to the bathroom to get ready for the day. By the time I emerged from our room, Emilia was about to explode with anticipation. She ran up to me as soon as I stepped foot out of our room.

"Lacey! Lacey! Santa was here!" She tugged on my hand and dragged me to the Christmas tree in the living room. There was a pile of presents under the tree.

"Wow! You're right. Let's wait for Uncle Blake to wake up and then we can open them," I said with a smile. Blake and I had brought out the presents late last night after Emilia went to bed.

He stumbled into the living room wearing his navy blue robe. His hair stuck up in all directions, making his head look like a porcupine.

"Look, Uncle Blake. Santa left us lots of presents."

Blake wrapped his arm around me and kissed the top of my head. "He sure did," he murmured.

"Can we open them now?" Emilia begged. She practically bounced on the tips of her toes in excitement.

One by one, we opened and exchanged our presents. Emilia tore through the wrapping paper on the first and biggest present. It was from Blake, and he had gotten her bunny dollhouse playset that was almost as tall as her. Next, Emilia opened my present.

"Bunny ears!" I helped her don the crocheted hat and tied the chin straps around her chin.

Those were her main presents. Her other presents included a large pillow-sized stuffed bunny as well as a bunny backpack and bunny school supplies. Given the events of this year,

Emilia opted out of preschool, but she was going to start kindergarten next year.

Next, it was time for me to open my presents.

"Emilia helped me pick both of them out," Blake said. He seemed nervous as I unwrapped it. Was he afraid I wasn't going to like what they got me? There was a black velvet box that looked like a necklace box. I gave him a quizzical look before I opened it. There was a gold and silver pen inside. Picking it up, I held the pen in my hand and savored the heavy weight for a moment before I put it back in the box carefully. It looked and felt expensive and I didn't want to drop it.

Quickly, I unwrapped the other item, revealing a thick leather bound journal. I stroked the soft leather cover wistfully. It was perfect. Finally, I had a nice notebook to jot down my ideas.

Blake tucked a finger under my chin and tipped my head up. "I can already hear your thoughts. Don't you dare hold back because you're afraid to mess up the journals. If I have to, I will buy every last journal and bit of stationery for you if that's what you need. Just write, Lacey."

My eyes grew moist. Nobody had ever known me like this. "Thank you, Blake, Emilia."

Emilia grinned up at me.

"I love it. I love you," I murmured.

"I love you too." He placed a gentle kiss on my lips. "Merry Christmas, my heart."

From her place on the floor next to the tree, Emilia giggled. "Your turn, Uncle Blake."

"Okay, let's see what we have." Blake retrieved the present I helped Emilia pick out. With careful precise motions, he removed the wrapping paper without tearing it.

He pulled out the mug and read the words on the side. World's Best Uncle Is A Sourdough Dealer. "Thank you, Emilia. I will use it for my coffee this morning."

Next, he opened the present I got him. My hands grew sweaty as I waited for him to reveal what was inside. Would he think it was stingy and cheap?

Blake unwrapped it with the same care as the other present. He opened the cardboard box and held up the little bread loaf ornament inside. The glass bauble was coated in a light layer of sparkling paint, making it glisten in the sunlight.

He laughed. "This is perfect, Lacey. I can't believe you actually found a bread ornament." With a pep in his step that rivaled his niece's energy, he sprung to his feet and found a bare spot on the tree to hang the ornament.

Blake picked Emilia up in his arms and joined me on the sofa. Emilia laid her head on my shoulder. "I know Santa really exists," she whispered in my ear.

I smiled. "Because he got you the dollhouse you wanted?"

She shook her head. "Because you're here with Uncle Blake. That's what I asked for. I love you so much, Lacey."

I pulled her tight against my chest. Over the top of her head, I met Blake's soft eyes. "Oh, sweetheart. I love you very much too. I will always be here with you. Forever."

EPILOGUE

LACEY

FIVE YEARS LATER

I leaned back in my chair and smiled as I watched Emilia play with little Xander around the Christmas tree. At nine years old, she was the perfect protective older sister to her little cousin. The two wolfling children were precocious and a handful at times, but I wouldn't trade it for the world.

It didn't take long for me to discover I was pregnant with our first child. After all, Blake had done everything to make sure that I was constantly bred since we first consummated our mating. My hand rested on top of my heavily round belly. This time next year, Emilia and Xander were going to have a little girl as another playmate. My heart fluttered as I pictured a group of rowdy kids playing around the Christmas tree. Blake said he was happy with however many children we ended up having, but I wanted more. I wanted laughter and chatter to fill this big house. In the future, when the children had their own families, we could build them their own homes on the estate. Lord knows the land was big enough to fit a small town.

Nanny Grace came in, resting her hands on her hips. She was stern, but sweet in the way she helped raise the kids. "Come along, children. It's time for breakfast, then you can open your presents."

With three children under the roof, Blake had finally convinced me to hire Grace before the baby arrived. At first, the thought pained me. Was I not a good enough mother to Emilia and Xander? But Grace lived up to her name, assisting me when I was too tired to chase after the kids without taking over as their mom.

And she arrived just in time. Not only was the baby due in three months, so was the manuscript for my next novel. My first novel became an overnight sensation when the book went viral online. After more than a year of negotiations, the new TV series based on the novel was going to come out next autumn.

At the promise of presents, Emilia and Xander followed Grace to the kitchen.

In this brief moment of stillness, I admired the giant decorated tree. All sorts of ornaments hung from its limbs. Joining the original bread ornament, there was a bookshelf ornament, and bunnies of all kinds for Emilia. Xander's favorite animals were owls, so we also had owls perched on the tree next to ornaments of the places we had traveled to as a family. It was a family tradition now to add a new ornament to our tree every year. I couldn't wait to see it overflowing with ornaments in the years to come.

Blake finally came back from the pool deck where he had been working on a Christmas barbecue. The weather this year was unusually warm in Huntington Harbor, and we decided to have a surf and turf meal instead of the usual Christmas ham.

"Reeve and Katie just called," he announced. "They're on their way over."

I rested my head on my headrest and smiled up at him. "It's going to be a full house here tonight." For the past couple of years, our best friends had spent the holidays at our home, but I had a feeling this was going to be the last Christmas we shared. Reeve didn't know it yet, but Katie was going to announce her pregnancy as a Christmas present to her mate today. I was sworn to secrecy and surreptitiously, I eyed the present under the tree. Reeve was going to be over the moon when he unwrapped it and found out he was going to be a daddy.

Blake kneeled next to my feet and rubbed his hands on my belly. The baby kicked as she recognized her father's touch.

"Tell me if you're tired. I can watch the kids while you rest."

"I'm fine," I insisted. Lifting my hand, I ran my fingers through his hair and scratched his head softly. The diamond on my wedding ring caught the sunlight in the window. "I'm just so happy."

Blake placed his head on my stomach. The baby kicked again.

"Me too," Blake murmured.

If I had one wish, it was always to be this joyful and content. I told Blake this.

He smiled up at me. "Oh, Lacey. This is just the start of our joy."

I agreed. In the meantime, I was going to have the best Christmas of my life so far with my family.

+++

Thank you for reading Billionaire Wolf Needs a Nanny.

Want to see what happens between Reeve and Katie? Check out the next book in the series, Billionaire Wolf Needs an Assistant (Reeve and Katie)

FREE BOOK: OWNED BY THE BILLIONAIRES

Fiona Bell will do anything to become a successful painter, even if it means working as a maid and practically being homeless. The last thing she needs is a distraction in the form of love. That is, until she finds herself trapped between two overbearing billionaires.

Alpha werewolves Huxley Cain and Derek Fox never expected to find a mate. That is until they meet her. From the moment they catch her sweet scent, they know she is the one to give them an heir.

They will stop at nothing to claim her.

She is theirs to protect.

Theirs to share in pleasure.

Theirs to claim together.

They will never let her go.

FIONA

I stood on my tiptoes and reached up until I could reach the top of the display case with my feather duster. Balancing on my toes carefully, I avoided touching the spotless glass with my fingers as I ran the duster across the top.

The last thing I wanted was to leave fingerprint smudges on the glass that I would have to clean again. It was nearly four o'clock, and I was almost done cleaning the house. I had a rare two hours booked at my school's painting studio, and I was never going to make it across the city in time if I didn't leave before rush hour traffic.

My reflection in the glass stared back at me. I paused, frowning at what I saw. Dark circles haunted my eyes and my hair was tied in a messy ponytail. The only thing I had going for me was a healthy pink flush across my bare cheeks from my physically demanding job as a maid.

My T-shirt was stretched out from washing with holes along the edges. The faded letters U and M of my university covered the area over my breasts.

The shorts I wore were tight and barely covered my bottom because they were already a couple of years old. I guess I had a late growth spurt and outgrew them in the last year. They were one of the few things I managed to take with me when my father cut me off and kicked me out of the house.

I was far away from being the pretty little socialite my father liked to parade around in front of his rich friends at parties. The way he used to show me off like a piece of meat made it obvious that he wanted to marry me off to one of their sons as soon as possible. I tugged on the edges of my shorts as I recalled how uncomfortable I used to be as the men, both young and old, would leer at my curvy figure. There were other rich people's sons and daughters at these parties, but I never really fit in with any of them. Every single party ended the same way, with me escaping as soon as possible and hiding out in the library or out near the kitchens with the servants.

I stabbed the furniture with force with the feather duster as I recalled the last argument I had with my dad.

For the crime of wanting to go to art school and wanting to be a painter instead of marrying his chosen protégé, the man I had looked up to my entire life cast me out to the streets.

"Selfish little whore, just like your mother."

His parting words still stung even after all these years. At eighteen years old, I had been abandoned once again, just like my mother abandoned me shortly after my birth.

Blinking rapidly, I cleared away the tears that stung my eyes.

None of that mattered now. Not only did I survive on my own, but three years later, I was thriving. I was going to graduate from U of M this year. And I did it all by myself, paying my way through college by cleaning rich people's houses. The only thing I needed to worry about was finishing school and getting my paintings into an exhibit.

A loud gurgle came from my stomach, reminding me that I skipped lunch. Ugh. I had to grab takeout on the way too. I had to finish cleaning up and get out of here.

I put in my earbuds and turned up the volume. The pounding beat of the music in my ears set the perfect pace for cleaning the rest of the room quickly. I sang along and shook my hips as I began to vacuum the room.

The giant bed in the center of the room was the toughest part to clean. It had to be wide enough for at least four people and the top of the mattress was strangely high, coming up to my tummy. I would need a step if I wanted to crawl up there.

My cheeks flushed as I suddenly realized why someone would need a bed like this. The bed was too high for someone as short as me, but it would be at groin height for a tall man. It was the perfect height for fucking. Not that I had any real-life experience with sex, but I had seen things online.

I shook my head and tried to get the perverted images out of my head. It was no business of mine what or who my boss did in his free time. It would be naïve to think that a man with his wealth wouldn't have women throwing themselves onto his bed.

Thankfully, I had never met my boss, or else the images in my mind would have been even more awkward. I had no idea who my employer was or what he looked like. Even though I had worked for him for more than three years, my only point of contact was with his personal assistant.

The mansion I cleaned gave away no clues. Everything was obviously expensive, from the multistory floor-to-ceiling windows overlooking the city below, to the infinity pool on the roof.

Even with all the luxury, the home was cold and sterile, strangely empty of all personal touches. Except for the custom bed in the master bedroom, of course. It could have been yet another home featured in those magazine articles about the mega rich and famous.

Getting down on my knees, I used the hose attachment on the vacuum to reach deep under the bed. My favorite song began and I swayed my hips as I vacuumed to the throbbing beat in my ears.

All I needed to know was that he was loaded and paid well for a clean home.

It was better this way.

There was no awkward conversation or pretending to listen and feigning concern about how hard it was to be so rich and powerful.

This way I could get my work done as quickly as possible. Best of all, I didn't need to care about what I looked like as I crawled around on my knees and bopped along to my favorite songs.

Suddenly, the vacuum cleaner lost power.

I frowned. That was strange.

It was then that I noticed the shadow that fell over the side of the bed.

Make that two shadows.

I froze. My hands shook as I plucked the earbuds out of my ears.

"Don't stop on our account."

The deep voice startled me. This was the first time I had ever run into another living person while cleaning this house. Now there were two strange men here. Suddenly, I remembered that I was on my knees with my ass in the air, and I was wearing a very short, very tight pair of shorts.

What must they think of me? My cheeks grew hot. I couldn't believe this was happening. This was not how I wanted to meet my boss and his guest.

I jumped to my feet. Eager to hide my barely covered ass, which was prominently on display, I spun around quickly.

To say the two men were gorgeous was an understatement. My breath caught in my throat as I admired their masculine features. Their slate colored suits molded to their muscles in all the right places. The one with dark hair carried an edge of danger to him, while the one with sandy blond hair quirked his lips in a sexy smirk. His eyes twinkled as he read my reactions like an open book.

Unfortunately, I was so focused on the twin sets of blue wolf-like eyes staring at me with hunger, that I failed to see where I was stepping. My foot caught on the edge of the fur rug next to the bed. I stumbled. As I fell, my arms flailed clumsily like a chicken flapping its wings in an attempt to regain my balance.

Tall, dark, and dangerous grabbed me, pulling me to his chest. I caught my breath and sighed at the warm, musky scent of the man holding me. To my surprise, the other man pinned me from behind, pressing the length of his hard body against my back.

Even as my heart hammered in my chest, I melted against the strong muscles cushioning me. In their overwhelming embrace, I was protected. I was safe.

I already thought they were huge from a distance. Now that they were up close, pressed against me, their size was almost beastly. Never in my life had I felt small or delicate like one of those waifish girls in the fashion magazines, but next to them, I was like a toy doll.

Their hands settled on my hips and waist. Heat spread from where their bodies touched mine, shooting straight to my core. I let out a whimper in desperate need. Despite my fear of their huge size, it all felt so right.

Never before had I ever felt this way. The sensations surging through my body were overwhelming and out of my control. There was nothing I could have done to stop the chain reaction I had to them.

I should have pushed them away. I should have screamed. They were too big. I should have been scared. They were too close, invading my space. But my body was warm and pliable while they held me. My limbs felt sapped of strength.

I brought a hand up to the muscular chest in front of me and flexed my fingers. Something primal in me wanted to dig my nails into his muscles. Instead, I pushed my palms against him, but it was useless. Neither of them budged an inch. Stuck between their hard chests and strong thighs, it was like pushing against a brick wall while being pinned in place by a boulder behind me.

The man behind me leaned down and buried his nose in my hair. He took a long deep breath and exhaled. His breath tickled the hairs on the back of my neck. My inner muscles clenched in need at the sensation.

"She's the one, Hux. She smells delicious." His low voice sent shivers up my spine.

Hux. Mr. Dark's name was Hux. It suited him.

"That's because she's ready for breeding." Hux's voice dripped with lust. He ran a thumb against my bottom lip. "A juicy, ripe peach that's ready to be eaten. So plump and sweet, I can't wait to take a taste."

"No!" This wasn't right. No matter what my traitorous body wanted, I couldn't let my first time be a quick and dirty threesome with my boss. I squirmed out from between them and held my hand out as if I could will them to stay away. "There will be no tasting of anything or anyone," I blurted. My voice cracked with panic as the words rushed out.

Hux barked out a deep laugh. "Our little rabbit's a feisty one, Derek." His eyes glinted with delight. "The chase is going to be so much fun."

My eyes flew to the other man. Derek grinned. A flash of fang peeked out from between his lips. There was something beastly about him. I blinked quickly. My eyes must have been playing tricks on me.

He ran his gaze up and down my body, stopping pointedly at my too-short shorts. His tongue ran across his bottom lip. I cursed at myself for choosing to wear them today. If I had remembered to do the laundry last weekend, I would have had clean clothes, then none of this would be happening.

I glanced between the two huge men to the door behind them. There was no way I could make it past them to my escape route.

I was trapped. A helpless rabbit ready to be ravaged by two savage beasts.

Read OWNED BY THE BILLIONAIRES

MATING SEASON SERIES

These alpha wolf pairs will stop at nothing to claim their mate when they catch her scent. She's in heat and ripe for breeding...

SERIES BOX SETS

Mating Season Collection 1 (Books 1-3)

Mating Season Collection 2 (Books 4-6)

Mating Season Collection 3 (Books 7-9)

Owned by the Billionaires (Fiona, Huxley, Derek)

Trick or Treat with the Billionaires (FREE only available at drusillaswan.com/newsletter) (Fiona, Huxley, Derek)

Captured by the Billionaires (Josephine, Samuel, Liam)

MATING SEASON SERIES

Mated to the Billionaires (April, Evan, Lawrence)

Kidnapped by the Billionaires (Sophie, Rick, Owen)

Stranded with the Billionaires (Amber, Nicholas, Constantine)

Taken by the Billionaires (Sarah, Mac, Callum)

Sold to the Billionaires (Beth, Troy, Sebastian)

Given to the Billionaires (Penny, Jake, Duncan)

Claimed by the Billionaires (Scarlet, Paxton, Austin)

FREE BOOK: SOLD TO THE MASTER VAMPIRE

The Doms of Darkness series begins with Alex and Amanda's story in Sold to the Master Vampire.

ONE CLICK TO GET Sold to the Master Vampire for FREE
GET THE COMPLETE SERIES: Doms of Darkness (The Complete Series: Books 1-4)
A master vampire takes what he wants, when he wants it.
The moment I saw her, I knew I had to have her.
The perfect pet.
Mine to tame. Mine to pleasure. Mine to protect.
A woman I could mold into my future queen.
But she's not as helpless as she seems.
Will she take her place as my mate?
Or will she lead me to my destruction?

I pushed my half-eaten chocolate raspberry mousse cake away and collapsed against the back of my seat. "I can't possibly eat another bite." The café where we had staked our claim smelled like dark roasted coffee, sugar, and cigarette smoke. I looked out the window and gazed lazily at the fashionable men and women walking down the street. They were so lucky to live here.

"You're such a lightweight, Amanda. Gimme." Meghan reached across the table and grabbed my plate. "I never want to leave Paris," she mumbled around a mouthful of mousse.

I don't know how she did it. We met at the hostel last week, and ever since then all we had done was sight see and eat. My new best friend and I had a plan to eat our way across the city before moving on to the next country on our Euro trip, where we were going to do the same thing all over again. While most tourists came to Paris for luxury shopping, we were here for the food and whatever tourist traps we could sneak into on a backpacking budget.

Suddenly, Meghan let out an ear-piercing scream. Her fork clattered to the floor, and she knocked over her cup of coffee. She clutched at her throat. Panic filled her eyes.

"Meghan!" I tried to reach across the table, but my arms moved like they were filled with lead. Her mouth opened and closed, but no words came out. Blood sprayed out between her fingers. The mist of blood splattered onto my face.

I jerked awake, falling back to reality from my dream of a life that didn't exist anymore. Every muscle and bone in my body ached from sleeping on the cold concrete floor. My stomach threatened to turn itself inside out from the smell of piss, blood, and vomit. Screams from several cells down the hall from mine bounced off the stone walls in a never-ending echo. There was a sickening thud and then it was silent.

My cellmate covered her ears and rocked back and forth with her head between her knees. I stood up on my tiptoes and peered out of the tiny street-level window in our cell.

It was futile, of course. Time had no meaning in this place. Once the vampires figured out how to get rid of the sun, it became impossible to tell how much time had passed. Even the moon disappeared without light from the sun. With nothing to light up the inky black sky, eternal darkness took over the world.

Keys jangled, and a metal door screeched in the distance. The hairs on my arms stood up in warning.

Not again.

I crawled back to the far corner of the cell and shrank down into the shadows as low as I could. I wrapped my arms around my knees and buried my face in my knees. If only the stone walls would swallow me up, so I could disappear. Silently, I prayed that they would ignore me and walk past my cell.

Heavy footsteps clomped down the hall, closer and closer. I made out two sets of footsteps. The guard who watched over the prisoners walked with a shuffling gait. The customer looking to buy a human from the merchandise on display in the dungeon walked with steady, sure steps. The human captives here were being sold off to vampires like cattle to be slaughtered. Whose turn was it going to be today?

The footsteps stopped suddenly. Male voices mumbled too softly for me to make out what they were saying. They were standing on the other side of the door.

I held my breath until my head pounded. Maybe if I kept perfectly still, they wouldn't see me.

"That one."

No, no, no, no.

The squeaky lock turned, and my cell door swung open with a groan. The guard came in first, followed by another vampire, who I guessed was today's buyer.

I darted my eyes around the room, looking for an escape route, but the two demons blocked the only way out of the room. The space closed in on us. Their large bodies took up all the room in the tiny cell.

The buyer was stylishly dressed, in a well-tailored gray silk suit that must have cost more money than I had in my bank account. His strong features were closed, revealing nothing about him. If I didn't know that he was a monster, I would have said that he was the most beautiful man I had ever seen.

The burly guard grabbed me by my arms and hauled me to my feet. I struggled, but it was less than useless. In fact, my resistance seemed to excite him. The demon tightened his grip painfully around my arms and flashed his fangs in my face. The smell of raw blood and decay was overwhelming. I was smelling the scent of his last meal. A captive just like me. My stomach turned violently. I wrenched myself out of his grasp and threw myself against the wall.

"Filthy whore!" The vampire guard growled and raised his hand to hit me. I squeezed my eyes shut, but the painful blow never came.

I opened my eyes and saw the guard's feet floating above the ground. The buyer had one hand wrapped around the guard's throat. The buyer flashed his fangs and his copper eyes glowed as he squeezed the guard's neck. Bone and tissue ground together, the noise echoing in the cell. Even though vampires didn't need to breathe, their flesh still bruised and their bones still broke. The guard clawed uselessly at the hand around his neck.

"You do not ever touch what is mine," he rasped around his fangs. He threw the guard to the other side of the room. My heart thudded at his strength and speed. His movements were quick, almost too quick to be seen with the human eye. The guard must have weighed over two hundred pounds, but the buyer tossed him aside like a crumpled ball of tissue without messing up his expensive suit. Despite his refined and regal exterior, there was no doubt that he was a warrior. A killer draped in fine silk.

"I-I'm sorry, Master Diamantis." The guard started to get up, but one look from the master vampire had him down on his knees again. The guard kept his eyes on the ground and bowed his head to the floor as he spoke, "She is to your satisfaction, Master?"

The master vampire paused to examine the goods he was buying. He swept his eyes up and down my body. Crossing my arms, I hugged my stomach. Though I could not imagine why. What he saw must have satisfied him.

"She will do. Have your sire arrange the settlement with my men."

"Yes, Master, anything you command." The guard cowered and bowed his head in subservience and backed out of the cell. Without giving me another glance, he backed out of the cell. He tripped over his feet, eager to get away from the powerful vampire.

I was all alone with the buyer now. Fear chilled my blood. I looked up into the cold, stony eyes of the vampire who bought me.

The vampire who was now my owner. My master. He was going to own and use me, and I was going to obey.

Or at least that's what I was going to make him think. As soon as I had a chance, I was going to make my escape.

GET SOLD TO THE MASTER VAMPIRE FOR FREE!

GET THE COMPLETE SERIES: Doms of Darkness (The Complete Series: Books 1-4)

ALSO BY DRUSILLA SWAN

If you want more by Drusilla, but you're not sure what to read next, here's a handy guide to help you pick your poison...

DOMINANT ALPHA MALES

All of my books

VAMPIRES

Doms of Darkness Series

Vampire Mafia Kings Series

Alien Vampires of Sangloria Series

MFM MENAGE

Mating Season Series

WEREWOLVES

Mating Season Series

My Grumpy Werewolf Boss Series

BILLIONAIRES

Mating Season Series

Indebted to the Billionaire Series

BRATVA MAFIA

Indebted to the Billionaire Series

ABOUT DRUSILLA SWAN

Steamy. Over-the-top. Alphas who claim their mates. Satisfying happily-ever-afters.

Join my newsletter at drusillaswan.com to get freebies and updates.

Find Drusilla at:

drusillaswan.com

Sign up for Drusilla's newsletter at:

drusillaswan.com/newsletter

Like Drusilla Swan on Facebook:

facebook.com/drusillaswan

Follow Drusilla Swan on Instagram

instagram.com/drusillaswanauthor

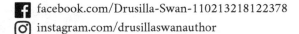

facebook.com/Drusilla-Swan-110213218122378
instagram.com/drusillaswanauthor

Copyright © 2024 by Drusilla Swan

All rights reserved.

No part of this book may be reproduced in any form or by any electronic or mechanical means, including information storage and retrieval systems, without written permission from the author, except for the use of brief quotations in a book review.

❦ Created with Vellum

www.ingramcontent.com/pod-product-compliance
Lightning Source LLC
LaVergne TN
LVHW090323160725
816300LV00004B/64